THE COURAGE CONSORT

The Courage Consort, possibly the seventh best-known a cappella vocal ensemble in Britain, are given two weeks in a Belgian chateau to rehearse their latest commission, the monstrously complicated *Partitum Mutante*. But is the piece performable? Does it matter that its composer is a maniac best known for attacking his wife with a stiletto shoe at the baggage reclaim of Milan airport? Can the five members of the consort endure their own sexual tensions and wildly differing temperaments? And what is the inhuman voice that calls out to them from the woods at night?

The esoteric world of avant-garde classical music is the unlikely setting for a story of rare power, perhaps the most moving Michel Faber has yet written. From the chaos and hilarity of *Partitum Mutante*, a numbed woman comes alive to the realities of friendship, independence and desire.

The Courage Consort

Michel Faber

CANONGATE BOOKS

...in 2001 by
Canongate Books Ltd, 14 High Street, Edinburgh EH1 1TE

This edition published in 2004

'Bohemian Rhapsody' Words and Music by Freddie Mercury
© 1975. Reproduced by permission of B Feldman & Co Ltd
trading as Trident Music, London, WC2H 0QY

British Library Cataloguing-in-Publication Data
A catalogue record for this book is available on
request from the British Library

ISBN 1 84195 5 345

Typeset by Patty Rennie Production, Portsoy
Printed and bound in Denmark by Nørhaven Paperback A/S

www.canongate.net

To all those who sing lustily and with good courage,
and to all who only wish they could.

My thanks, as ever, to Eva, especially for her help
in creating the characters of Ben and Dagmar

THE COURAGE CONSORT

ON THE DAY THE GOOD NEWS ARRIVED, Catherine spent her first few waking hours toying with the idea of jumping out the window of her apartment. Toying was perhaps too mild a word; she actually opened the window and sat on the sill, wondering if four storeys was enough to make death certain. She didn't fancy the prospect of quadriplegia, as she hated hospitals, with their peculiar synthesis of fuss and boredom. Straight to the grave was best. If she could only drop from a height of a thousand storeys into soft, spongy ground, maybe her body would even bury itself on impact.

'Good news, Kate,' said her husband, not raising his voice though he was hidden away in the study, reading the day's mail.

'Oh yes?' she said, pressing one hand against the folds of her dressing-gown to stop the chill wind blowing into the space between her breasts.

'The fortnight's rehearsal in Martinekerke's come through.'

Catherine was looking down at the ground far below. Half a dozen brightly-dressed children were loitering around in the car-park, and she wondered why they weren't at school. Then she wondered what effect it would have on them to see a woman falling, apparently from the sky, and bursting like a big fruit right before their eyes.

At the thought of that, she felt a trickle of mysterious natural chemical entering her system, an injection of something more effective than her anti-depressants.

'Is . . . is it a school holiday, darling?' she called to Roger, slipping off the sill back onto the carpet. The Berber plush felt hot against her frigid bare feet, as if it had just come out of a tumble-dryer. Taking a couple of steps, she found she was numb from waist to knee.

'School holiday? *I* don't know,' her husband replied, with an edge of exasperation that did not lose its sharpness as it passed through the walls. 'July the sixth through to the twentieth.'

Catherine hobbled to the study, running her fingers through her tangled hair.

'No, no,' she said, poking her head round the door. 'Today. Is today a school holiday?'

Roger, seated at his desk as usual, looked up from the letter he was holding in his hands. His reading glasses sat on the end of his nose, and he peered forbearingly over them. His PC's digital stomach emitted a discreet *nirp*.

'I wouldn't have the foggiest,' he said. At fifty-two years old, a silver-haired veteran of a marriage that had remained carefully childless for three decades, he obviously felt he'd earned the right to be hazy on such details. 'Why?'

Already forgetting, she shrugged. Her dressing-gown slipped off her naked shoulder, prompting one of his eyebrows to rise. At the same moment, she noticed *he* wasn't in pyjamas any longer, but fully dressed and handsomely groomed. Hitching her gown back up, she strained to recall how she and Roger had managed to start the day on such unequal footing. Had they got up together this morning? Had they even slept together, or was it one of those nights when she curled up in the guest bedroom, listening to the muted plainsong of his CDs through the wall, waiting for silence? She couldn't remember; the days were a chaos in her brain. Last night was already long ago.

Smiling gamely, she scanned his desk for his favourite mug and couldn't spot it.

'I'll put the kettle on, shall I?' she offered.

He produced his mug of hot coffee out of nowhere.

'Some lunch, perhaps,' he said.

Determined to carry on as normal, Roger picked up the telephone and dialled the number of Julian Hind.

Julian's answering machine came on, and his penetrating tenor sang: *'Be-elzebub has a devil put aside for me-e-e . . . for me-e-e . . . for meeeeeeee!'* – the pitch rising show-offishly to soprano without any loss of volume. Roger had learned by now to hold the telephone receiver away from his ear until the singing stopped.

'Hello,' said the voice then, 'Julian Hind here. If *you* have a devil put aside for me, or anything else for that matter, do leave a message after the tone.'

Roger left the message, knowing that Julian was probably hovering near the phone, his floppy-fringed head cocked to one side, listening.

★

Next, Roger dialled Dagmar's number. It rang for a long time before she responded, making Roger wonder whether she'd gone AWOL again, mountain-climbing. Surely she'd have given that a rest, though, in the circumstances!

'Yes?' she replied at last, her German accent saturating even this small word. She didn't sound in the mood for chat.

'Hello, it's Roger,' he said.

'Roger who?' There was a horn-like sonority to the vowels, even on the telephone.

'Roger Courage.'

'Oh, hallo,' she said. The words were indistinct amid sudden whuffling noises; evidently she'd just clamped the receiver between jaw and shoulder. 'I was just talking to a Roger. He was trying to sell me some thermal climbing gear for about a million pounds. You didn't sound like him.'

'Indeed I hope not,' said Roger, as the nonsense prattle of Dagmar's baby began to google in his ear. 'This is to do with the fortnight in Martinekerke.'

'Let me guess,' said Dagmar, with the breezily scornful mistrust of the State – any State – that came to her so readily. 'They are telling us blah-blah, funding cuts, current climate, regrets . . .'

'Well, no, actually: it's going ahead.'

'Oh.' She sounded almost disappointed. 'Excellent.' Then, before she hung up: 'We don't have to travel together, do we?'

After a sip of coffee, Roger rang Benjamin Lamb.

'Ben Lamb,' boomed the big man himself.

'Hello, Ben. It's Roger here. The fortnight in Martinekerke is going ahead.'

'Good. Sixth of July to twentieth, yes?'

'Yes.'

'Good.'

'Good . . . Well, see you at the terminal, then.'

'Good. 'Bye.'

Roger replaced the receiver and leaned back in his swivel chair. The score of Pino Fugazza's *Partitum Mutante*, which, before the calls, had been glowing on his PC monitor in all its devilish complexity, had now been replaced by a screen-saver. A coloured sphere was ricocheting through the darkness of space, exploding into brilliant fragments, then reassembling in a different hue, over and over again.

Roger nudged the mouse with one of his long, strong fingers. Pino Fugazza's intricate grid of notes jumped out of the blackness, illuminating the screen. The cursor was where Roger had left it, hesitating under something he wasn't convinced was humanly possible to sing.

'Soup is served,' said Catherine, entering the room with an earthenware bowl steaming between her hands. She placed it on his desk, well away from the keyboard as she'd been taught. He watched her as she was bending over; she'd put a T-shirt on underneath her dressing-gown.

'Thanks,' he said. 'Any French rolls left?'

She grinned awkwardly, tucking a lock of her greying hair behind one ear.

'I just tried to freshen them up a bit in the microwave. I don't know what went wrong. Their molecular structure seems to have changed completely.'

He sighed, stirring the soup with the spoon.

'Five to ten seconds is all they ever need,' he reminded her.

'Mm,' she said, her attention already wandering outside the window over his shoulder. Meticulous though she could be with musical tempos, she was having a lot of trouble lately, in so-called ordinary life, telling the difference between ten seconds and ten years.

'I do hope this chateau is a *cheerful* place,' she murmured as he began to eat. 'It would have to be, wouldn't it? For people in our position to bother going there?'

Roger grunted encouragingly, his face slightly eerie in the glow of the monitor through the haze of soup-steam.

Roger Courage's Courage Consort were, arguably, the seventh most-renowned serious vocal ensemble in the world. Certainly they were more uncompromising than some of the more famous groups: they'd never sunk so low as to chant Renaissance accompaniment to New Age saxophone players, or to warble Lennon/McCartney chestnuts at the Proms.

A little-known fact was that, of all the purely vocal ensembles in the world, the Courage Consort had the highest proportion of contemporary pieces in their repertoire. Whereas others might cruise along on a diet of antique favourites and the occasional foray into the twentieth century, the Courage Consort were always open to a challenge from the avant-garde. No one had performed Stockhausen's *Stimmung* as often as they (four times in Munich, twice in Birmingham and once, memorably, in Reykjavik) and they always welcomed invitations to tackle new works by up-and-coming composers. They could confidently claim to be friends of the younger generation – indeed, two of their members were under forty, Dagmar Belotte being only twenty-seven. Fearlessly forward-looking, they were already signed up for the Barcelona Festival in 2005, to sing a pugnaciously post-millennial work called *2K+5* by the *enfant terrible* of Spanish vocal music, Paco Barrios.

And now, they had been granted two weeks' rehearsal time in an eighteenth-century chateau in rural Belgium, to prepare the unleashing of Pino Fugazza's fearsome *Partitum Mutante* onto an unsuspecting world.

♫♫♫

Come the sixth of July, the early-morning English air was still nippy but the Belgium midday was absolutely sweltering. The message from God seemed to be that the Courage

Consort shouldn't be deceived by the brevity of the plane and train journeys or the trifling difference in geographical latitude: they had crossed a boundary from one world into another.

In the cobbled car-park outside Duidermonde railway station, an eleven-seater minibus was waiting, its banana-yellow body dazzling in the sun. Behind the wheel, a smart young man was keeping an eye out for British singers through a pair of very cool granny specs. He was Jan van Hoeidonck, the director of the Benelux Contemporary Music Festival. Spotting his overdressed guests disembarking from the train, he flashed the headlights of the minibus in welcome.

'The Courage Consort, yes?' he called through the vehicle's side window, as if to make perfectly sure it wasn't some other band of foreign-looking travellers lugging their suitcases through the railway barriers.

Benjamin Lamb, towering over the others, waved in salute. He was grinning, relieved there had been no turnstiles to squeeze through – the bane of his travelling life. The mighty scale of his obesity was easily the most identifiable feature of the Courage Consort, though if anyone who'd never met them before asked for a pointer, Roger would always tactfully advise: 'Look out for a man with silver-grey hair and glasses' – himself, of course.

'But aren't there supposed to be five of you?' asked the director as Roger, Catherine, Julian and Ben approached the side of the minibus.

'Indeed there are,' said Roger, rolling open the sliding door and heaving his wife's huge suitcase inside. 'Our contralto is coming under her own steam.'

Jan van Hoeidonck translated this idiom into Dutch instantaneously, and relaxed behind the wheel while the Consort lugged their belongings. Catherine thought he seemed a friendly and intelligent young man, but was struck by his apparent lack of motivation to come out and help. *I'm in a foreign country*, she told herself. It hadn't been real to her until now. She always slept like a corpse on planes and trains, from the moment of departure to the instant of arrival.

Having loaded his luggage next to hers, Roger walked jauntily round the front of the vehicle and got in next to the director. He consulted no one about this. That was his way.

Catherine climbed into the banana-yellow bus with her fellow Courage Consort members. In true British fashion, each of them sat as far away from the others as possible, spreading themselves across the nine available seats with mathematical precision. Ben Lamb needed two seats to himself, right enough, for his twenty stone of flesh.

Catherine looked aside at Julian. It had been three months since she'd seen him, or so Roger said. It seemed more like three years. In profile, his heavy-lidded, supercilious face, superbly styled black hair and classic cheekbones were like a movie star's, with the same suggestion of jaded, juvenile naughtiness. He might have been the older brother she never had, contemptuously running ahead of her to the haunts of grown-up vice but never quite escaping her memories of him in short trousers and shopping-centre haircut. Yet he was only thirty-seven, and she was ten years older than that.

As the bus pulled away from the station, Catherine reflected that she almost always felt much younger than other people, unless they were clearly minors. This wasn't vanity on her part; it was inferiority. Everyone had negotiated their passage into adulthood except her. She was still waiting to be called.

Jan van Hoeidonck was talking to her husband in the front. The director spoke as if he'd been facilitating cultural events since World War II. But then they all spoke like that, Catherine thought, all these cocky young administrators. The chap at the Barbican was the same — born too late to remember the Beatles, he talked as if Peter Pears might have cried on his shoulder when Benjamin Britten died.

Self-confidence was a funny thing, when you thought about it. Catherine squinted out the window, stroking her own shoulder, as the bus ferried them into a surreally pretty forest. Chauffeured like this, towards a nest prepared for her by admirers, she still managed to feel like a fraud; even under a shimmering sun, travelling smoothly through placid woodland, she felt a vapour of fear breaking through. How was that possible? Here she was, an artist of international standing, secretly wondering whether she looked dowdy and feeble-minded to Jan van Whatsaname, while he, a fledgling bureaucrat with the pimples barely faded from his pink neck, took his own worth for granted. Even

Roger listened respectfully as Jan explained his plans to steer the ship of Benelux art into new and uncharted waters.

'Of course,' Jan was saying, as the minibus delved deeper into the forest, 'multi-media events are not so unusual with rock music. Have you seen Towering Inferno?'

'Ah . . . the movie about the burning sky-scraper?' Roger was more of a Bergman and Truffaut man himself.

'No,' Jan informed him, 'they are a multi-media music group from England. They have performed a piece about the Holocaust, called *Kaddish*, all over Europe – and in your own country also. The piece used many video projections, an orchestra, the Hungarian singer Marta Sebestyén, many things like this. I hope this piece *Partitum Mutante* will do something similar, in a more classical way.' The director slowed the vehicle and tooted its horn, to scare a pheasant off the road. They had encountered no other traffic so far. 'Wim Waafels,' he went on, 'is one of the best young video artists in the Netherlands. He will visit you here after a week or so, and you will see the projections that you will be singing under.'

Julian Hind, listening in, remarked:

'So, we'll be the Velvet Underground, and this video chap will be Andy Warhol's *Exploding Plastic Inevitable*, eh?'

Roger glanced over his shoulder at Julian in mute incomprehension, but the director nodded and said 'Yes.' Catherine had no idea what any of this was all about, except that Roger didn't like being shown up on matters musical.

Catherine's chest tightened with disappointment as, true to form, her husband took his paltry revenge. She tried to concentrate on the lovely scenery outside, but she couldn't shut her ears to what he was doing: moving the conversation deftly into the area of European arts bureaucracy, a subject Julian knew next to nothing about. He reminisced fondly about the French socialist administration that had made the 1985 Paris Biennale such a pleasure to be involved with, and expressed concern about where the management of the Amsterdam Concertgebouw was heading just now. Catherine's irritation softened into boredom; her eyelids drooped in the flickering sunshine.

'So,' interrupted the director, evidently more concerned about where the conversation was heading than the fate of the Concertgebouw. 'This Consort of yours is a family affair, yes?'

Catherine's ears pricked up again; how would her husband handle this? Nobody in the ensemble was actually a Courage except her and Roger, and she tended to cling to her maiden name as often as she could get away with it, for sheer dread of being known as 'Kate Courage'. She couldn't go through the rest of her life with a name like a comic-book super-heroine.

Suavely, Roger more or less evaded the issue.

'Well, believe it or not,' he said, 'the Consort is not specifically named after me. I regard myself as just one member of the ensemble, and when we were trying to think of a name for ourselves, we considered a number of things, but the concept of courage seemed to keep coming up.'

Catherine became aware of Julian's head tilting exaggeratedly. She watched an incredulous smirk forming on his face as Roger and the director carried on:

'Did you feel maybe that performing this sort of music needs courage?'

'Well . . . I'll leave that to our audiences to decide,' said Roger. 'Really, what we had in mind was more the old Wesleyan adage about hymn-singing, you know: "Sing lustily and with good courage".'

Julian turned to Catherine and winked. '*Did* we have that in mind?' he murmured across the seats to her. 'I find myself strangely unable to recall this momentous conversation.'

Catherine smiled back, mildly confused. While meaning no disloyalty to her husband, she couldn't recall the conversation either. Turning to look out the window of the minibus, she half-heartedly tried to cast her mind back, back, back to a time before she'd been the soprano in the Courage Consort. Hundreds of neat, slender trees flashed past her eyes, blurring into greeny-brown pulsations. This and the gentle thrumming of the engine lulled her, for the third time today, to the brink of sleep.

Behind her, Benjamin Lamb began to snore.

For the last couple of miles of their journey, the chateau was in plain, if distant, view.

'Is that where we're going?' asked Catherine.

'Yes,' replied Jan.

'The wicked witch's gingerbread house,' murmured Julian for Catherine to hear.

'Pardon?' said the director.

'I was wondering what the chateau was actually called,' said Julian.

'Its real name is 't Luitspelershuisje, but Flemings and visitors call it Chateau de Luth.'

'Ah . . . Chateau de Luth, how nice,' repeated Catherine, as the minibus sped through the last mile – or 1.609 kilometres. When the director parked the car in front of the Consort's new home-away-from-home, he smiled benignly but, again, left them to deal with their own baggage.

The Chateau de Luth was more beautiful, though rather smaller, than Catherine had expected. A two-storey cottage built right next to the long straight road between Duidermonde and Martinekerke, with no other houses anywhere about, it might almost have been an antique railway station whose railway line had been spirited away and replaced with a neat ribbon of macadamised tar.

'Luciano Berio and Cathy Berberian stayed here, in the last year they were together,' said the director, encouraging them all to approach and go inside. 'Bussotti and Pousseur too.'

The house was in perfect condition for its age, except for the artful tangle of stag horns crowning the front door, which had been eaten away somewhat by acid rain in the late Eighties. The red brick walls and dark grey roof tiles were immaculate, the carved window-frames freshly painted in brilliant white.

All around the cottage, lushly tasteful woodland glowed like a high-quality postcard, each tree apparently planted with discretion and attention to detail. Glimpsed among the straight and slender boughs, an elegant brown doe froze to attention, like an expensive scale model of a deer added as a *pièce de résistance*.

Catherine stood gazing while Roger took care of her suitcase somewhere behind her.

'It all looks as if Robin Hood and his Merry Men could trot out of the greenery any minute,' she said, as the director ambled up.

'It's funny you say this,' he commented. 'In the Sixties there was a television series filmed here, a sort of French Robin Hood adventure called *Thierry la Fronde*. This smooth road through the forest was perfect for tracking shots.'

The director left her deer-spotting and hurried off to unlock the front door, where the others stood waiting. They were arranged in a tight trio around their bags and cases, Ben at the back and the shorter men in front, like a rock group posing for a publicity shot.

Jan worked on the locks, first with a massive, antique-looking brass key and then with a couple of little stainless-steel numbers.

'Presto!' he exclaimed. Never having seen a conjurer at work, Catherine took the expression as a musical directive. What could he want them to do *presto*? She was in a somewhat *adagio* state of mind.

The chateau's magnificent front room, all sunlight and antiques, was obviously the one where rehearsals would take place. Julian, as he was wont to do, immediately tested the acoustic with a few *sotto voce* Es. He'd done this in cellars and cathedrals from Aachen to Zyrardów; he couldn't help it, or so he claimed.

'Mi-mi-mi-mi-mi,' he sang, then smiled. This was a definite improvement on Ben Lamb's rather muffled sitting room.

'Yes, it's good,' smiled the director, and began to show them round.

Catherine had only been inside a couple of minutes when she began to feel a polite unease finding a purchase on her shoulders. It wasn't anything to do with the atmosphere of the place: that was quite charming, even enchanting. All the furniture and most of the fixtures were dark-stained wood, a little sombre perhaps, but there was plenty of sunlight beaming in through the many windows and a superb smell, or maybe it was an *absence* of smell: oxygen-rich air untainted by industry or human congestion.

All cons, both mod and antique, were on offer: Giraffe upright piano, electric shower, embroidered quilts, microwave oven, fridge, a concert-sized xylophone, an eighteenth-century spinning-wheel, two computers, a complete pre-war set of Grove's *Dictionary of Music and Musicians* (in Dutch), an ornate rack of wooden recorders (sopranino, descant, alto, tenor, plus a flageolet), several cordless telephones, even an assortment of slippers to wear around the house.

No, it wasn't any of these things that troubled Catherine as she accompanied her fellow Consort members on their guided tour of the chateau. It was entirely to do with the number of bedrooms. As the director escorted them from one room to the next, she was keeping count and, by the time he was showing them the galley kitchen, a burnished-wood showpiece worthy of Vermeer, she appreciated there wasn't going to be any advance on four. One for Ben, one for Julian, one for Dagmar, and . . . one for herself and Roger.

'The shops are not so accessible,' the director was saying, 'so we've put some food in the cupboards for you. It is not English food, but it should keep you alive in an emergency.'

Catherine made the effort to look into the cupboard he was holding open for their appraisal, so as not to be rude. Foremost was a cardboard box of what looked, from the illustration, exactly like the vegetation surrounding the house. '*BOERENKOOL*', it said.

'This really is awfully sweet,' she said, turning the almost weightless box over in her hands.

'No,' said Jan, 'it has an earthy, slightly bitter taste.'

So there were limits to his ability to understand his visitors from across the channel, after all.

♩♩♩♩♩

It was around nine o'clock in the evening, almost nightfall, when Dagmar finally showed up. The director had long gone; the Courage Consort were busy with unpacking, nosing around, eating Corn Flakes ('Nieuw Super Knapperig!'), and other settling-in activities. It was Ben who noticed, through an upstairs window, the tiny cycling figure approaching far in the distance. They all went to stand outside, a welcoming committee for their prodigal contralto.

Dagmar had cycled from Duidermonde railway station with a heavy rucksack on her back and fully laden baskets on both the front and rear of her bicycle. Sweat shone on her throat and plastered her loose white T-shirt semi-transparently against her black bra and tanned ribcage; it darkened the knees of her electric-blue sports tights and twinkled in the unruly fringe of her jet-black hair. Still she seemed to have plenty of energy left as she dismounted the bike and wheeled it towards her fellow Consort members.

'Sorry I took so long; the ferry people gave me a lot of hassles,' she said, her huge brown eyes narrowing slightly in embarrassment. Like all colourful non-conformists, she preferred to zoom past awed onlookers, leaving them gaping in her wake, rather than be examined at leisure as she cycled towards them over miles of dead flat road.

'Not to worry, not to worry, we've not started yet,' said Roger, stepping forward to relieve her of the bicycle, but it was Ben she allowed to take it from her. Despite his massive size, unfeasible for cycling, she trusted him to know what to do with it.

Swaying a little on her Reebok feet, Dagmar wiped her face with a handful of her T-shirt. Her midriff, like all the rest of her skin, was the colour of toffee.

'Well, childbirth hasn't made you any less of an athlete, I see,' commented Julian.

Dagmar shrugged off the compliment as ignorant and empty.

'I've lost a hell of a lot of muscle tone, actually,' she said. 'I will try to get it back while I'm here.'

'Toning up!' chirped Julian, straining, as he always did within minutes of a reunion with Dagmar, to remain friendly. 'That's what we're all here for, isn't it?'

The thought of Dagmar's eight-week-old

baby roused Catherine from her daze. 'Who's taking care of little Axel?' she asked.

'It's not a problem,' Dagmar replied. 'He's going to be staying here with us.'

This revelation made Julian's chin jut forward dramatically. Accepting delivery of Dagmar had already sorely taxed him; the prospect of her baby coming to join her was just too much to take.

'I . . . don't . . . know if that would be such a good idea,' he said, his tone pensive and musical, as if she'd asked him his opinion and he had deliberated long and hard before responding.

'Is that so?' she said coldly. 'Why not?'

'Well, I just thought, if we're being given this space – this literal and metaphysical space – to rehearse in, far away from noise and distractions, it . . . well, it seems odd to introduce a crying baby into it, that's all.'

'My baby isn't a very crying baby, actually,' said Dagmar, flapping the hem of her T-shirt with her fists to let the cooling air in. 'For a male, he makes less noise than many others.' And she walked past Julian, to stake her own claim to the Chateau de Luth.

'Well, we'll find out, I suppose,' Julian remarked unhappily.

'Yes, I guess we will,' Dagmar called over her shoulder. On her back, nestled inside her bulging rucksack, a spiky-haired infant was sleeping the sleep of the just.

By the time the Courage Consort settled down to their first serious run-through of *Partitum Mutante*, dark had come. The burnished lights cast a coppery glow over the room, and the windows reflected five unlikely individuals with luminous clarity. To Catherine, these mirrored people looked as if they belonged together: five Musketeers ready to do battle.

If she could just concentrate on that unreal image, shining on a pane of glass with a forest behind it, she could imagine herself clinging onto her place in this little fraternity. The rehearsals were always the hardest ordeal; the eventual performance was a doddle by comparison. The audience, who saw them presented on stage as if they were a projection from far away, knew no better than that they were a closely-knit clan, and this allowed them to behave like one. The artificiality of the concert platform was insulated against disturbing events: no one argued, or sulked, or asked her questions she couldn't answer, or expected her to say yes to sex. All they did was sing, in perfect harmony. Or, in the case of Pino Fugazza's *Partitum Mutante*, perfect disharmony.

'F sharp there, Kate, not F natural.'

'Honestly?'

'That's what's written. On *my* print-out, at least.'

'Sorry.'

The trick was lasting the distance from now till the première.

♪♪♪♪♪

Late on the first night in the Chateau de Luth, tucked up in a strange, soft bed next to Roger, Catherine turned the pages of *Extended Vocal Techniques* by the Extended Vocal Techniques Ensemble of California. It was a book she resorted to sometimes to put her to sleep, but tonight it had the additional purpose of keeping physical contact off the agenda.

Roger was reading a coffee-table book on Karel Appel, a Dutch artist, that he had found in a bookshelf downstairs – or rather he was looking at the pictures, she supposed; she didn't think her husband had managed to learn Dutch for this adventure. He *might* have done, but she imagined she'd have noticed something if he had.

Slyly she glanced at him from time to time, without moving her head. He was sinking further down in the bed, inch by inch. Her almost invincible insomnia would give her the edge soon enough, she hoped. She read on.

'Vowels can be defined linguistically by the characteristic band of overtones each contains. These bands are narrowed to specific pitches, so that the singer's voice resonates in a way that reinforces a single harmonic partial of the fundamental being sung. Such reinforced harmonics make it possible to write in eight parts for four singers.[3]

Catherine wondered if, rather than losing her sanity, she was perhaps merely getting old.

'Crazy character, this Karel Appel,' remarked Roger.

'Mm,' she said, drawing her knees up a little under the quilted eiderdown to better support her book. She wished this new piece by Pino Fugazza didn't require her and Dagmar to do so many things that distorted normal perception. Other people might think it was terribly exciting when two females singing in thirds made the airwaves buzz weirdly, but Catherine was finding that her nerves were no longer up to it. Even the way a sustained A flat tended to make an auditorium's air-conditioning hum gave her the creeps lately. It was as if her face was being rubbed in the fact that music was all soundwaves and atoms when you stripped the Baroque wrapping-paper off it. But too much sonic nakedness wasn't good for the spirit. At least that's what she was finding lately, since she'd started coming . . . adrift. A bit of Bach or Monteverdi might be more healing than what this Pino Fugazza expected of her.

Cowardly sentiments, she knew, from a member of the Courage Consort.

When Roger finally fell asleep, it was long past midnight. She didn't know exactly what time, because the only clock in the room was Roger's watch, hidden underneath his pillow as he breathed gently off the edge of the bed. It was strange the things you forgot to bring with you to a foreign place.

Catherine laid *Extended Vocal Techniques* gingerly on the floor, drew the eiderdown up to her chin, and switched off the bedside light. The silence that descended on her then was so uncompromising that she was unnerved by it. It was as if the whole universe had been switched off.

On the threshold of sleep, she found herself wondering how a person might go about killing herself in an environment like this.

At dawn, there were birds. Nothing on too grand a scale, just a few piccolo chirps and twitterings from species unknown. How strange that in London, in her flat near the half-dozen trees planted by the council, there should always be such a racket in the mornings from throngs of birds making the best of things, while here, in the middle of a forest, so few voices should be raised. Either there were only a handful of birds out there, chirping at the tops of their lungs in a hopeless attempt to fill the vacuum, or else there were millions and millions of them, all keeping silent. Sitting in the branches, waiting for the right moment.

Catherine was aghast to find herself becoming afraid: afraid of all the millions of silent birds, infesting the trees, waiting. And, knowing how irrational this fear was, she despised herself. Surely she was too crazy to live, surely it was high time she cleaned herself off the face of the planet, if she'd sunk to feeling anxiety even at the thought of birds sitting contentedly in a forest. It was as if the frayed and tangled wiring of her soul, submitted to God for repairs, had been entrusted to incompetent juniors instead, and now she was programmed to see danger in every little sparrow, dire warning in music, deadly threat from the love of her own husband.

Roger was sleeping like a stone beside her. He might wake any second, though; he never snuffled or fidgeted before waking, he just opened his eyes and there he was, fully conscious, fully functioning. Catherine looked at his head on the pillow, the head she'd once been barely able to resist stroking and kissing in adoration. She'd been so grateful he wanted her, so in awe of his conviction that he could shape her into something more than just another lost and self-destructive girl with a pretty soprano voice.

'You've got it inside you,' he'd promised her.

Yearning, terrified, she'd left her father's house at long last, and given herself over to Roger Courage instead.

Now she lay next to him in this strange soft bed in Belgium, and she wished she could breathe some magic odourless chloroform into his open mouth, to keep him safely asleep while she worked up the courage to face the day.

She mentioned the unearthly silence of the night to the others, over breakfast. She was light-headed with relief by then: she'd leapt out of bed and got herself ready before Roger was able to rouse himself from an unusually deep sleep. She was already in the kitchen, fully dressed, before he made his way downstairs to join his fellow Consort members. She was cooking *haver-mout* – porridge by any other name – for a ravenous unshaven Ben, and generally behaving like a sound-minded person.

'Good morning, darling,' she said, as her husband appeared. He looked a bit nonplussed, padding down the stairs in his herringbone-patterned socks. (All the men were in socks, actually, caught between the chateau's house rule against wearing shoes and their own reluctance to wear the leather clogs provided for them.)

Julian, bleary-eyed and elegantly dishevelled, was nursing a coffee without drinking it. As soon as Catherine mentioned the silence, he said he'd noticed it too, and that it wasn't natural. He'd lain awake all night because of it.

Catherine shuddered; the thought of her and Julian lying awake at exactly the same time in the same house, with only a wall between them, was disturbing somehow. It wasn't that she disliked him really, but she was so thin-skinned nowadays, so hypersensitive, that this simultaneous insomnia in a shared darkness was like unwelcome intimacy.

'And the way there's hardly any birdsong, in this big forest: that's a bit unsettling, don't you think?' she suggested hesitantly, wary of stepping into the spotlight of mental frailty but enjoying the idea of communication with her friends.

Dagmar was cutting fresh bread on the kitchen worktop, her snoozing baby lying swaddled in a blanket on the same surface, right near the breadboard, as if she meant to slice him next.

'That silence is what you get if you climb a mountain,' she said, referring to her favourite pastime. 'I like it.'

Having failed to get any joy from womankind, Catherine looked back to the men. Ben was now busy with the *havermout*, however, spooning it through his big soft lips, and Julian had turned his attention to his coffee, so that left only Roger.

Her husband searched his soul briefly for some appropriate observation.

'A vocal acoustic as silent as this must be very rare, when you think about it,' he said. 'I mean, just think of that recording of Hildegard songs by Gothic Voices . . . There you have Emma Kirkby singing like a lark, and in the background you can hear cars accelerating along the road!'

Julian had to disagree.

'That's because the sound engineers placed the microphones such a long way back from the singers,' he said, 'to try and get that monastery acoustic. They should have miked the singers close up, and put some reverb on later.'

'You can't mean that,' protested Roger. Catherine had ceased to exist, forgotten as she tried to make toast for him under the oven grill. 'The acoustics of a place are unique and precious.'

'For a live performance, yes,' agreed Julian. 'I've never sounded better than in that cellar in

Reykjavik, with the stone walls and everything. But Gothic Voices weren't performing, they were making a record. Who needs the Church of St Jude-on-the-Wall in Hampstead if at the flick of a switch or the push of a fader you can have a churchy acoustic, without the bloody Volvo vrooming up the road?'

A smell of burnt toast started to pervade the kitchen. Little Axel coughed uneasily and started flapping his arms gently on the kitchen worktop, as if trying to fly away to a fresher square of air.

'Sorry,' said Catherine.

♪♪♪♪♪

Partitum Mutante was sheer pleasure for at least one of its performers: Benjamin Lamb. Pino Fugazza was obviously very taken with the sonorous chanting of Tibetan monks, and had written oodles of something very similar for the bass parts of his own piece.

While the other members of the Courage Consort had to learn complicated and athletic melodies in perverse keys, Benjamin was required to hum like an organ for bar after bar after bar. At the very beginning of the piece, his vocalisations were intended to convey the birth of the universe, no less, and he tackled this with an eerie resonance worthy of a holy Himalayan – indeed, of several.

'Mwoooooiiiinnng, mwoooooiiiiinnng, mwoooooiiiiinnng,' he sang, from deep within his huge belly.

Pino Fugazza was cunning, though: he'd timed low baritone swoops for Roger to cover Ben's pauses for breath, creating the illusion of a ceaseless foghorn of bass. And, just when it seemed that the music was going to remain abyssally dark forever, Julian came in with a high, pure voicing of the first articulate word: 'God' – pitched in G major, of course.

The real trouble came with the entry of the females, a reflection no doubt on the Italian's philosophy of human relations as filtered through Judeo-Christian tradition. The manuscript became alarmingly complex at this point, the notes crowding the bar lines like dense troops of ants squashed wholesale on the way to something irresistible.

Dagmar and Catherine sang till the sweat was falling off their brows onto the pages. They sang until their throats ached. They sang until they both felt moved to stare at each other imploringly, like two plantation slaves willing each other not to collapse, for that would be to invite a far worse fate. The hours were passing, not in linear flow, but in endless repetitions of two minutes here, five minutes there, and then the same two minutes from before, over and over and over.

Finally, as night was again falling, the Consort reached the end of the piece, and, one by one, each of the singers faded away, leaving Catherine to bring *Partitum Mutante* to its close. The very last note was a very high C, to be reached over several bars from two octaves below, then sustained for fifteen seconds, increasing in volume, then diminishing to nothing. Ecstatic that the end was in sight, Catherine sang it with the purity and sureness of a fife.

For several seconds after she had ushered the last traces of the note into oblivion, the rest of the Courage Consort sat mute. In the extraordinary quiet of Martinekerke forest, they breathed like babies, no one wanting to be the first to speak.

'I was worried about that one, I must confess,' said Roger, finally. 'Well done.'

Catherine blushed and concealed her throat behind one hand.

'I just seem to be able to hit higher and higher notes all the time,' she said.

The silence moved in again, as soon as she'd finished speaking, so she pressed on, making conversation to fill the void.

'Maybe if I'd had one of those fearsome Svengali mothers pushing me when I was young I could have been a coloratura by now.'

Dagmar was uncrossing her lotused legs with a wince of discomfort, wiggling her naked feet – her own solution to the house slipper dilemma.

'So what sort of mother did you have?' she asked.

Catherine looked up at the ceiling, to see what might be written there about what sort of mother she'd had.

'She was a cellist, actually,' she replied meditatively, 'in the BBC Symphony Orchestra.'

'But I meant what sort of person was she?'

'Umm . . . I'm not really sure,' murmured Catherine, her vision growing vague as she stared at the delicate mosaic of cracks in the paint overhead. 'She was away a lot, and then she committed suicide when I was twelve.'

'Oh, I'm sorry,' said Dagmar.

It sounded odd, this effete Britishism, coming at robust volume from the German girl. The sharpness of her accent made the condolence sound like something else altogether, and yet there was nothing insincere in her tone: in fact, it was Dagmar's sincerity that really struck the discord. The phrase 'Oh, I'm sorry' must have been composed by the English to be softly sung in a feminine cadence.

'Not your fault,' said Catherine, lowering her gaze to smile at Dagmar. A ghostly blue after-image of the ceiling lamp floated like an aura around the German girl's face. 'It was me who found her, actually. Me or I? – which is it, Roger?' She glanced at him, but not long enough to notice his frowning, eyebrow-twitching signal for her to stop talking. 'She did it in her bed, with sleeping pills and a polythene bag over her head.'

Dagmar narrowed her eyes and said nothing, imagining the scene and how a child might have taken it in. Julian couldn't contain himself, however.

'Did she leave a note?' he enquired.

'No,' said Catherine. Roger was getting up,

rustling papers at the periphery of her attention. 'Though the polythene bag wasn't a plain one. It was a UNICEF one, with pictures of smiling children all over it. I always wondered about that.'

Even Julian couldn't think where to take the conversation from there.

'Tragic business,' he said, getting to his feet to follow Roger into the kitchen.

Dagmar wiped her forehead with one arm. As she did so, the fabric of her top was pulled taut against her breasts, alerting her to the fact that she had leaked milk from her nipples.

'Excuse me,' she said.

'How long has it been, do you think,' enquired Roger in bed that night, 'since we last made love?' Leading a singing group, he'd learned to hide his fault-finding under a consultative guise.

'I don't know,' she said truthfully. 'Quite a long time, I suppose.' It would have been . . . undiplomatic to suggest otherwise, obviously.

The spooky silence of Martinekerke forest was back with them in the inky-black bedroom. Catherine wondered what had become of the moon, which she could have sworn was almost full last night. There must be clouds hiding it just now.

'So, do you think we might have a problem?' said Roger after a while.

'I'm sure it's nothing that won't come good,' said Catherine. 'The doctor did say that the anti-depressants might suppress . . . you know . . . desire.' The word sounded cringe-makingly romantic, a Barbara Cartland sort of word, or else a throwback to William Blake.

> *What is it that women do require?*
> *The lineaments of gratified desire.*

It was partly to save her from having to figure out what such terms as 'lineaments' could possibly mean that Catherine had originally allowed Roger to pluck her out of Magdalen's College.

'Are you still listening to me?' he prompted now, in the vacuum of the noiseless night.

'Yes,' she assured him. 'I was just thinking.'

'Thinking what?'

'I can't remember now.' She giggled in embarrassment.

Roger lay still for another few seconds or

minutes, then rolled onto his side – facing her. Not that she could see his face, but she could feel his elbow digging into the edge of her pillow and could sense, in the centre of the bed near her own thighs, the warmth of his . . . well, his desire.

'You're still a good-looking woman, you know,' he said in a quiet, deep voice.

Catherine laughed out loud, unable to control herself. The faint praise, offered so solemnly, so seductively, at a time when neither of them could see a bloody thing, struck her as unbearably funny somehow.

'I'm sorry, I'm sorry,' she whispered, mortified lest Julian hear them through the wall. 'It must be the anti-depressants.'

Roger slumped onto his back with an emphasis that rocked the bed-springs.

'Maybe you should stop taking them now,' he suggested wearily. 'I mean, have you felt suicidal lately?'

Catherine stared out of the window, relieved to see a pale glow of moonlight seeping into the sky.

'It comes and goes,' she said.

Hours later, when he was asleep, Catherine

began to weep in the silence. She wished she could sing to herself, something sweet and tuneful, a little Schubert *lied* or even a nursery rhyme. 'Twinkle, Twinkle, Little Star' would do fine. But of course it wasn't possible. Her throat was sore from singing *Partitum Mutante*, and she lay in dread of waking her husband, in a strange bedroom in a forest in Belgium, with that wicked Julian Hind listening through the wall for her every snuffle. Oh my God, how had things come to this?

Suddenly, she heard a short, high-pitched cry from somewhere quite far away. It wasn't Axel, she didn't think; that boy slept like an angel all night through and, during the day, hardly uttered a sound unless you set fire to a slab of Belgian bread right near his nose.

Catherine's skin prickled electrically as the cry came again. It didn't sound human, or if it was, it was halfway towards something else. She wished she could slide across the bed, into the big protecting arms of someone who could be trusted to do nothing to her except keep her warm and safe. Such people were hard to find, in her experience.

Instead, she drew the bedclothes up to her

mouth and lay very still, counting the cries until she fell asleep.

♫♫

In the morning, she didn't manage to make an appearance at breakfast. She'd hoped to be there, bright-eyed and bushy-tailed, each morning before Roger, but the previous night's insomnia caught up with her and she slept till midday. Roger was long gone by the time she awoke. Score: Roger: one, Catherine: zero, then.

The sun was pouring in through the window, its heat boosting her body's metabolism to an itchy simmer. Just before waking, she'd been having a nightmare of suffocation inside a humid transparent sac; anxiously conscious at last, she fought her way out of the clammy bedclothes and sat up, drenched with sweat.

She showered and dressed, hearing nothing except the sounds she herself was making. Perhaps the others were sitting around downstairs, waiting to sing, but lacking their soprano. Perhaps they'd gone exploring together, leaving her alone in the Chateau de Luth with its spinning-wheels and antique recorders and a bed she didn't know if she could bear to lie in again.

She needn't have worried. Arriving in the kitchen, she found Ben still in his XXL pyjamas, looking slightly sheepish as he sat alone at the sunlit bench, browsing through a four-year-old *Times Literary Supplement*.

He was such a strange man, Catherine thought. The oldest of them all, he was as baby-faced at fifty-five as he'd been when the Courage Consort first formed. He'd always been immense, too, though perhaps marginally bigger now than a couple of decades ago. Quietly competent and poised in every sphere of life, he had just this one area of weakness, his Achilles' stomach. Each concert tour brought more surprises from his store of hitherto unsuspected talents – last year he'd dismantled the engine of a broken-down tour bus and got it going with a necktie and two wedding rings – but he just wasn't terribly good at feeding himself.

'Hello,' he said, and a rumbling noise not a million miles removed from the moans he contributed to *Partitum Mutante* issued from somewhere inside him.

Catherine had no doubt he could have solved whatever physical and intellectual challenges a cooking pot and a box of oats might pose, but, plainly, there was some reason why he couldn't bring himself to tackle them. He looked at Catherine, his eyes sincere in their supplication. He was telling her, with that look, that he loved his own wife dearly, but that his wife was in London and Catherine was here with him, and what were they going to do about it?

'Would you like some porridge, Ben?' she asked him.

'Yes,' he immediately replied, colour rising to his great cheeks.

'Then I'll make us both some,' she said.

It turned out that the Courage Consort had already been lacking its contralto even while its soprano slept the morning away. At first light, Dagmar had cycled off into the forest with Axel, and had not yet returned. Perhaps she'd gone to Martinekerke or Duidermonde to fetch more supplies; perhaps she was merely exercising. She was gone, anyway, so Roger was typing corre-spondence on one of the computers, Julian was reading a paperback in the sitting room, and Ben had been waiting around for someone to offer him breakfast.

'Say "whoa",' said Catherine as she began to pour the milk.

'Whoa,' he murmured regretfully, when the bowl threatened to overflow.

Overhearing the sounds of nurture, Julian found his way back to the kitchen, where he'd fed himself on tinned rice pudding and coffee a few hours earlier. He was dressed in black jeans, a black T-shirt, black socks. From the top of his blow-dried head to where his ankles began, he looked like a French film star.

'Morning,' he grinned, still holding his book aloft, as if he'd just glanced up from his reading and noticed the kitchen had sidled up to him.

'Hello Julian,' said Catherine, trying not to be sour-faced as the moment of benign simplicity – the bowl of hot oatmeal, herself as provider, Ben Lamb as mute recipient – was ruined. As Julian stepped casually between herself and Ben, she noted that the book spread-eagled in his elegant hands was some sort of thriller with a frightened female face on the cover, and she suddenly thought, *I really, really dislike this man.*

'Julian, would you like some porridge?'

During the first five words of her question his eyes lit up, but they dulled in disappointment when she reached the end.

'No thanks,' he said. 'There's nothing . . . ah . . . more substantial is there?'

'I don't know,' said Catherine, gazing wistfully at Ben spooning the steaming *havermout* into his mouth. 'Porridge is quite filling, isn't it?'

'I was thinking of eggs, actually,' confessed Julian.

'Perhaps Dagmar will bring some back with her.'

'Mm.' Plainly, for Julian, the prospect of asking Dagmar to share food with him was not a realistic one.

Scraping the remnants of the *havermout* into a bowl for herself, Catherine asked Julian how he'd slept.

'Lay awake half the night again,' he grumbled, settling himself on a stool. His paperback nestled on his lap, its glossy image of a wide-eyed beauty staring up from between his slim black thighs.

'You heard the cries, then?' said Catherine.

'Cries?'

'Cries, out there in the forest somewhere.'

'Probably Dagmar's baby,' he suggested. 'Or bats.'

She could tell he hadn't heard anything really.

'I definitely heard them,' said Catherine. 'Human. But terribly forlorn and strange. Just cries, no words.'

Julian smiled indulgently.

'An infant crying in the night,/an infant crying for the light,/and with no language but a cry, eh?' he said, deadpan.

Catherine stared at him in uneasy puzzlement. Julian often came out with this sort of thing: a tantalising quote from one of her favourite Victorian or Romantic poets, delivered with a shrug as if it were an arch soundbite from a TV commercial or an election slogan of yesteryear made tacky, or poignant, or poignantly tacky, by hindsight.

Elsewhere in the house, a telephone rang.

'Ghostbusters,' quipped Julian.

The call was from a young woman called Gina. She wanted to know if it was convenient for her to drive over this afternoon and clean 't Luitspelershuisje, change the bed linen, that sort of thing.

Catherine was relieved when Roger told her

this. She hadn't expected domestic help some-how; after the director's indifference to their baggage, she'd assumed it wouldn't be Dutch. But if someone could come and do something about the sweat-soaked sheets on the bed she'd have to share with Roger tonight, that would make a big difference.

Minutes after Roger passed on the message about the maid, Dagmar returned from her adventures, hot and bothered. She barged into the kitchen, plastic bags in each fist, Axel still on her back. He was whimpering and grizzl-ing.

'*Moment mal, moment mal,*' she chided him, dumping groceries on the kitchen bench. The *Times Literary Supplement* was obscured by yoghurts, fresh apricots, crispbreads, cheeses, avocados, cold meats, coffee, cartons of 'Vla met echt fruit!', plastic flip-top containers of baby-wipes – and eggs.

Roger was already gone; Ben Lamb followed him gracefully, recognising that there wasn't room in the kitchen for all this bounty, Catherine, Dagmar, Julian, and himself as well. Julian hesitated, his eyes on the eggs. He was thinking he might be able to put up with the irritating noise of the baby if there were omelettes on the horizon.

But Dagmar sat heavily on a stool right opposite him and hoisted Axel over her shoulder, depositing him on her lap. Then, hitching her T-shirt up, she uncupped one breast and guided her baby's mouth to the nipple.

'Excuse me,' said Julian, leaving the women to it.

Catherine sat at the kitchen bench, staring abstractedly into Ben's porridge bowl. It was so clean and shiny it might have been licked, though she imagined she would have noticed if that were the case. She herself tended to half-eat food and then forget about it. Roger didn't like that for some reason, so, back home in London, she'd taken to hiding her food as soon as she lost her appetite for it, in whatever nook or receptacle was closest to hand. *I'll finish this later*, she'd tell herself, but then the world would turn, turn, turn. Days, weeks later, ossified bagels would fall out of coat pockets, furry yoghurts would peep out of the jewellery drawer, liquefying black bananas would lie like corpses inside the coffins of her shoes.

She hoped she wasn't doing it here in the Chateau de Luth, though chances were that she was. Roger was probably cleaning up after her, refraining from saying anything because of the other people. Could she perhaps be getting Alzheimer's instead of going crazy? At forty-seven she doubted it was very likely . . . Still: there was something so very blameless and . . . non-negotiable about Alzheimer's. Nobody would think of telling you to pull yourself together, or get impatient for you to return to your sex life. You wouldn't have to take Prozac anymore, and if somebody found a hoard of half-eaten apples behind the television, well, they'd understand.

And when you died, you wouldn't even know what was happening. You'd just dither absent-mindedly into the next world, blinking mildly in the light of the Almighty.

Catherine's eyes came into focus on the *Times Literary Supplement*, from which she had removed the food and neatly put it away in refrigerator and cupboards minutes ago. The *TLS* was open at the letters pages, and nine distinguished academics from all over Britain and the USA were arguing about the dedicatee of Shakespeare's sonnets, taking it all very personally. *Correspondence on this matter is now closed*, warned the editor, but after nigh-on four hundred years it was pretty obvious that the sonnets argument, like all arguments, would run forever without resolving anything. As for Catherine, she had no opinion, except that it would be nine different kinds of Hell to be married to these men.

'You can eat any of the food that you want,' Dagmar said.

Catherine had forgotten the German girl was there, and looked up with a start.

'Oh . . . thank you,' she said.

'Except if I'm the only one of us who's going to be shopping, I'll need to have some extra money soon,' added Dagmar. Her baby was still sucking at the breast, placid as a sleeping kitten.

'Just mention it to Roger, he'll take care of it,' said Catherine. She hadn't signed a cheque or set foot in a bank in years. Latterly she had a little plastic card which gave her money out of a slot in the wall, providing she could remember a four-digit number – and the card, of course. There was nowhere in Martinekerke forest where that little plastic card could be inserted.

'How did you sleep last night, Dagmar?' asked Catherine, carrying Ben's bowl to the sink.

'Perfect,' said Dagmar.

'You didn't hear anything unusual, in the small hours of the morning? Like a cry from the forest?'

'Nothing wakes me,' said Dagmar, looking down at Axel, 'except him, of course.'

This seemed unlikely, given the child's almost noiseless functioning, but Dagmar must know what she was talking about. Catherine was struck by how, when the German girl was looking down at the baby at her breast, her slim, taut-skinned face acquired a double chin, adding five years to her age. There was a pale scar on Dagmar's forehead, too, which Catherine had never noticed before. Wrinkles of the future, cicatrices of the past, all the million marks recording a private life that no outsider could ever understand.

'Are you enjoying yourself here?' asked Catherine.

'Sure,' Dagmar replied. 'It's good they provide us with this space. I've been a professional musician now for ten years, and I have a kid; it's about time somebody pays for us to rehearse, yeah?'

'But the place itself, and the piece itself – are you enjoying those?'

'I don't care at all about Pino Fugazza's music,' shrugged Dagmar, removing Axel from her breast. Saliva gleamed on her nipple and areola, prompting immediate loss of eye contact from Catherine. 'I want to sing it well. If I get too bored with the music put in front of me, I should get off my ass and compose some of my own, yeah?'

Catherine, still embarrassed at her own queasiness about the spittly nipple, was even more thrown by this turn the conversation was taking. The American-accented 'ass' instead of 'arse' emphasised Dagmar's foreignness even more than her German accent usually did, and her frank indifference to the commission that had brought them all here was startling. Strangest of all was this notion that you could compose yourself, if you were dissatisfied with the music you were given.

'You write music?' At the bottom edges of her vision, Catherine registered that the T-shirt was coming down, covering the perturbing swell of flesh.

'Sure,' said Dagmar, finding a more convenient spot to lay her boy's wispy head. 'Don't you?'

Catherine had never once dreamt of composing a note. She played the piano competently, could get by on the flute, could hear a piece of music playing in her head just by reading the score – though not as accurately as Roger could hear it, of course. When it came to score-reading, she imagined her brain as an old radio, fading out now and then, and Roger's brain as a CD player, extracting every nuance with digital efficiency. As for the prospect of making her *own* marks on the staves: no, that was inconceivable. The only times she ever sang a note that was different from what had been written for her, Roger was always there to say, "F sharp, Kate, not F natural," or whatever.

'I'm sure I don't have what it takes,' she told Dagmar.

The German girl wasn't passionately motivated to disagree, her brown eyes as dark and opaque as Belgian mocha chocolate.

'If you think so,' she shrugged.

Catherine flinched inwardly: she'd been hoping for reassurance. How strange these Germans were, not understanding that a declaration of unfitness was really a plea for encouragement. Perhaps it was a good thing they hadn't won the Battle of Britain.

'I haven't had the right training, for a start,' Catherine said. 'People like Pino Whatsisname have studied composition for years and years.'

Dagmar was plainly unawed by this reminder of Pino's credentials.

'Humming to yourself in the bath is composing, don't you think?' she said, hugging Axel up onto her shoulder. 'I sing to myself when I'm out cycling, and to my kid. It's not *Partitum Mutante* I'm singing, that's for sure.'

She grinned, and Catherine grinned too. It was a nice, safe place to leave the conversation.

'I'm going to put Axel to bed now,' said Dagmar. 'You should go out for a walk, don't you think? Everything is perfect out there — the weather, the forest, everything.'

'I'd like that,' promised Catherine. 'I really would. But maybe Roger wants us to start now.'

The look she got from Dagmar then was enough to shame her into finding her shoes.

★

Gina the maid arrived in a little white Peugeot just as Catherine was stepping out the door — excellent timing, since it meant that Roger couldn't be angry about the delay in the rehearsals, could he?

Slightly awed at her own daring wayward-ness, Catherine cast off from the house without even explaining herself to anyone, hurried into the fringe of the forest, then peered through the sparse trees back at the chateau. Roger and Julian were competing to welcome Gina, who, contrary to expectations, was a blonde twen-tysomething with a figure like a dancer and work apparel to match. Everything in the Netherlands was of better quality than you thought it would be. Even the vacuum cleaner that Gina was struggling to remove from her vehicle's back seat without the assistance of foreigners looked like a design award-winner that could suck anything into its sleek little perspex body.

To the best of Catherine's knowledge, Roger had never been unfaithful to her. It wasn't his style. Once he made a commitment to some-thing, he stuck with it and never let go, no matter what. No matter what. Nor was a sudden heart attack or stroke likely to take him from her. He was four years older than her, but very fit. They would be together always, unless she died first.

Catherine turned her back on the chateau and wandered deeper into the trees. As she walked she kicked gently at the soft, rustling carpet of fallen leaves and peaty earth, to leave some sort of trail she could follow later if she got lost. The sky was clear, the breeze gentle. Her footsteps would remain, she was sure.

During the war, the Nazis had probably killed people in these woods. The war had come to Belgium, hadn't it? She was vaguely ashamed to concede that she wasn't sure. She didn't really know much about anything except singing. Roger had rescued her from post-adolescent misery at Magdalen's College and, forever after, had taken responsibility for the world at large. He told her what he thought might interest her, vetted out what in his opinion she'd rather not know. Then again, she was terribly forgetful, especially lately. Roger possibly *had* told her about Belgium and World War II once, but she would have forgotten it by now.

Anyway, assuming there *had* been Nazis in

this forest, this would have been a perfect spot to execute people. Catherine wondered what it would be like to be rounded up, herded to the edge of a communal grave, and shot. She tried to feel pity for those who didn't wish to die: women with children, perhaps. All she could think of was what a mercy it would be to have the burden of decision shouldered by someone else: a Nazi to lead you from prevarication to the grave, where he would shoot you in the back of the head, a place you couldn't reach yourself.

Then, a few years later, a French Robin Hood and his Merry Men would ride their horses over your bones, twirling their colourful pennants, delighting children all over Europe.

After fifteen minutes or so, Catherine stopped walking and squatted against the mossy bough of a cedar, making herself comfortable on the forest bed. The ground was quite safe to rest her bottom – her ass? – on; it seemed to have been designed by Netherlandish scientists to nourish vegetation without staining trousers. The warmth of the sun, diffused by the treetops, beamed vitamin D onto her skin. All around her, pale golden light flickered subtly on the greens and browns, the leaves breathing out their clean, fragrant oxygen.

Composers are often inspired by nature, she thought. Beethoven's '*Pastoral*' *Symphony*, Vaughan Williams, Delius, that sort of thing. What did nature mean to her? She tried to decide, as if God had just asked her the question.

Nature meant the absence of people. It was a system set up to run without human beings, concentrating instead on the insensate and the eternal. Which was very relaxing now and then. But dangerous in the long run: darkness would fall, and there would be no door to close, no roof over one's head, no blankets to pull up. One wasn't an animal, after all.

Catherine stood up and slapped the leaves and fragments of bark off the seat of her jeans. She'd had enough nature for one day. It was time she was getting back to the house.

Walking back along the path she'd made, she became aware of all the birds that must be sitting in the trees all around and above her. A few were twittering musically, but the vast majority were silent. Looking down at her. It didn't bear thinking about; she concentrated on the sound of her own feet rustling through the undergrowth.

Her quickening breathing sounded amazingly loud in the stillness, and as she walked faster the breaths became more like voiced utterances, with an actual pitch and timbre to them. Exactly like avant-garde singing, really: the vocalisations of a terrorised soul.

She was almost running now, stumbling on loose branches and clods of earth she had kicked up earlier. The sunlight was flickering much too fast through the trees, like malfunctioning fluorescence, lurid and cold. Had she lost track of time again? Was she hours away from home?

What would she do if she heard the cry?

The thought came suddenly, like an arrow shot into her brain. She was alone in the forest of Martinekerke with whatever had wailed out to her during the night. Its eyes were probably on her right now, glowing through the trees. It was waiting for the right moment to utter that cry again, waiting until she had blundered so close that it could scream right in her ear, into the nape of her neck, sending her crashing to her knees in panic. Catherine ran, whimpering anxiously. She would be a good girl from now on, if only Roger would come and rescue her.

Breathless, half-blind, she broke into the clearing. For all the intensity of her dread, she'd taken only a couple of minutes to put the forest behind her; she hadn't strayed very far from home at all. The chateau was right there across the road, and the little white Peugeot parked outside spoke of the impossibility of supernatural cries.

'OK, time for *Partitum Mutante*,' said Roger to her, as soon as she stepped across the threshold.

♫♫♫♫

Rehearsals went badly that day. Ben, Dagmar and Catherine were game enough, but Roger was irritable, strangely unsettled. Julian had his mind on something else and lost his place in the score at every small distraction – like Gina leaving the house, for example. He watched her through the sparkly clean windows as she loaded her equipment into her car, and his cue to sing the words of the Creator God went by unnoticed.

Politely hostile words between Julian and

Roger were mercifully interrupted by another phone-call. It was a journalist from a Luxembourg newspaper, trying to find a story in the Benelux Contemporary Music Festival.

Those members of the Consort who were not Roger Courage sat idle while Roger handled the enquiries, the first of which was evidently why Pino Fugazza's piece was called *Partitum Mutante*. This was one of many questions that Catherine had never thought to ask Roger, so she made the effort to listen to his reply.

'Well, my Italian is pretty rudimentary,' he purred into the mouthpiece, implying quite the opposite, 'but I gather the title isn't Italian as such, or even Latin. It's more a sort of multi-layered pun on lots of things. There's a play on *partita*, of course, in the sense of a musical suite, as well as some reference to *partum*, in the sense of birth. *Mutante* then suggests mutant birth, or a mutant musical form . . .'

Catherine's attention wandered to the forest outside. A deer was grazing right near the window. It was really awfully nice out there, seen from indoors. She must go walking in the woods more often, face her fears, not be such a baby.

'I do think it's awfully important to give performers of newly commissioned music adequate rehearsal time,' Roger was saying to the journalist from Luxembourg. 'Too often when you go to a première of a contemporary vocal work, you're hearing singers flying by the seat of their pants, so to speak, on a piece they've only just learnt. There hasn't been time to master it fully, to capture the nuances and inflections. You have to remember that when a traditional vocal group sing Handel's *Messiah* or some such chestnut, they can virtually sing it in their sleep. What we, in the Courage Consort, are trying to do with *Partitum Mutante* here in this splendid chateau is learn it to the point when we can sing it in our sleep. That's when the real work can begin.'

Moments later, when Roger was off the phone and sitting down with his fellow Consort members, Catherine said:

'I thought it meant underpants.'

Dagmar chuckled throatily, a release of tension. Roger looked at his wife as if he had every expectation that she would resume making sense very soon, if he only stared hard enough into her eyes.

'*Mutante*,' Catherine explained. 'I could've sworn it meant underpants.'

'I'm sure it's to do with mutation, dear,' Roger warned her mildly, rolling his eyes from side to side to remind her they were not alone in their apartment now. But she was not to be brushed off like that. She had been to Italy only last year, singing Dowland and Byrd. En route, she'd done a bit of shopping in Rome, thrilled and terrified to be off Roger's leash for an hour.

'I remember when I was in Rome,' she said, 'I needed some briefs. I was in a big department store and I didn't know how to ask. Obviously I couldn't show them my knickers, could I? So I looked up underpants in a guide book. I'm sure it said *mutante*.' She laughed, a little embarrassed. 'That's the sort of thing I do remember.'

Roger smirked wearily.

'On that note,' he said, 'coffee, anyone?'

When they were all sitting together again, Roger informed them that Pino Fugazza himself would be paying a visit to them tomorrow, to see – or rather hear – how they were progressing with his masterpiece. What needed to be discussed before then, obviously, was which parts of *Partitum Mutante* they needed to rehearse most intensively, in order to make the best possible impression on the composer.

It was a tense discussion, at least among those of the Consort who had an opinion on the matter. Julian felt the tenor-rich passages were most underdeveloped, while Dagmar was sure that the contralto and soprano harmonics were far short of ideal; Roger tended towards the view that these weaknesses could be improved at leisure within a binding framework woven by a clean and confident baritone line. An impasse was reached with no singing done. Julian went to the toilet, Roger went for a breath of fresh air, and Dagmar went to look in on Axel.

Left alone with Ben, Catherine said:

'I've still got the briefs, actually. They lasted superbly. I might even have them on right now.'

Ben rested his massive head on his hands and half-closed his eyes, smiling.

In bed that night, Roger finally allowed himself to be badly behaved.

'You don't love me anymore,' he said, as Catherine cringed beside him, rolling herself up into a ball.

'I don't know, I don't know,' pleaded Catherine, her voice strangled to a squeak by tears and too much singing.

'Have you given any more thought to stopping the anti-depressants,' he enquired tonelessly, tugging at the blankets to cover the parts she had exposed.

'I've already stopped,' she said. It was true. It had been true for days. In fact, despite Roger's frequent gentle reminders, back in London, about all the items she should make sure she took with her to Belgium, she had somehow managed to leave those little pills behind. The cardboard box they lived in had got beetroot and mayonnaise soaked into it somehow, and she hadn't been up to fixing the problem. The box of pills, the spilled food, the handbag in which all this had happened: she'd left the whole caboodle under her bed at home. The bed she slept in alone, in the spare room.

'Really?' said Roger, lying right next to her in Belgium. 'So how are you feeling?'

She burst out laughing. She tried desperately to stop, mindful of Julian in the next room, but she couldn't; she just laughed louder, sobbing until her sides were aching.

Later, when the fit had subsided, Roger lay with his head and one hand against her back.

'We have a big day tomorrow,' he sighed, heavy with loneliness on the brink of sleep.

'I won't let you down,' Catherine assured him.

No sooner had his breathing become deep and regular than the first cry echoed eerily in the forest outside.

♫♫♫♫

'Come for a cycle with me,' Dagmar invited her next morning after breakfast.

Catherine blushed, her hands trembling up to her throat. She could not have been more nonplussed if she'd just been asked to go skinny-dipping in Arctic waters with a bunch of fervent Inuits.

'Ah . . . it sounds lovely, Dagmar, really, but . . .'

She looked to Ben for help, but he was busy spooning up the *havermout*, content as a . . . well, a lamb.

'I haven't got a bicycle, for one thing,' she pointed out gratefully.

'I found one at the back of the chateau,' said Dagmar. 'It's an old one, but sound construction. A good Dutch bike. But if you think you can't ride an old one, you can use mine.'

Defeated, Catherine allowed herself to be led out of the house. The German girl's thighs and buttocks flexed like an Olympian's as she walked, the shiny aquamarine of her tights contrasting sharply with the pastel blue of Catherine's evenly faded jeans. There were the two bicycles already parked, side by side at the edge of the road, gleaming in the sun. There was no escape except to say *No, I don't want to*, which had always been impossible for Catherine.

'They say you never forget how to ride a bicycle,' she said, approaching the machines warily, 'but I've forgotten the most amazing things, you know.'

'It's all right, we'll take it easy,' said Dagmar, preoccupied with strapping on the Axel ruck-sack.

Catherine examined the seats of the two bikes, feeling the leather curves, trying to imagine how hard or soft each might be between her legs.

'Erm . . . which of these is better for someone who hasn't . . . you know . . .'

Dagmar shrugged, quite an achievement for a woman with a six-kilo human being on her back.

'One bike has about a hundred gears, the other has none,' she said. 'But travelling slow on a totally flat road, it makes very little difference.'

And so it began. Catherine's anxiety turned to relief as she discovered she could still ride perfectly well. Her other fear, that Dagmar would speed ahead of her, was equally unfounded. The German girl cycled at a slow and even pace – not because she was making any special effort to be considerate, but because she had simply sent an instruction down to her legs to rotate at a certain number of revolutions per minute. Whatever the reason, Catherine was able to keep up, and, to her growing delight, found herself cycling along the dark smooth road, forest blurring by on either side, a breeze of her own creation blowing through her hair.

After a mile or two, she was even confident enough to speak.

'You know, I really am enjoying this terribly much,' she called across to Dagmar.

Axel, nestled against his mother's back, his face barely distinguishable under a woollen cap, opened his eyes wide. He wasn't used to fellow travellers.

'You will sing better tonight,' Dagmar asserted confidently. 'It's good for the lungs, good for the diaphragm, good for everything.'

'You'll have me going mountain climbing with you next!' It was the sort of comment you could make in the Low Countries, without fear.

'Great idea,' called Dagmar. 'There are some OK mountains just over the German border, in Eifel. Three hundred kilometres' journey, maximum.'

Catherine laughed politely, possibly not loud enough for Dagmar to hear over the whirring of the wheels. In the distance, a church spire gave advance warning of Martinekerke.

It was a proud and glowing Catherine who cycled up to the front door of the Chateau de Luth an hour later. She had been exploring the big wide world, making a bit of a reconnaissance of the local facilities. Now she and Dagmar were bringing back the goodies.

The three men watched them mutely as they, two flushed and sweaty women, carried groceries into the kitchen.

Mind you, Catherine hadn't actually been able to carry much on the bicycle with her, having neglected to bring along any sort of bag. But she'd taken responsibility for the eggs, wrapping them up in a sweater she was too hot to wear, and nestling them safely in the basket of her strange Dutch bike.

'You may need another shower, dear,' Roger suggested *sotto voce* as she was pouring a big glass of milk down her glistening throat. 'Pino Fugazza will be here soon.'

Abruptly, for no apparent reason, little Axel started bawling.

Of all the composers that the Courage Consort had ever met, Pino Fugazza proved to be the least charming. Perhaps they ought to have been forewarned slightly when they'd found out that his sizeable fortune derived not from the honest popularity of avant-garde music but was inherited from the family business of automatic weapons. However, in a spirit of not blaming the child for the sins of his parents, they reserved judgement. In any case, as Ben pointed out, Tobias Hume, a favourite composer of the Courage Consort's seventeenth-century repertoire, had actually been a professional killer in his time, and that didn't detract from the merit of the songs he'd written for the viol.

The image of a dashing Tobias Hume laying sword aside to pen the immortal 'Fain would I change that note' was rudely extinguished by the very real arrival, in a black Porsche, of Pino Fugazza. He swanned into the chateau wearing a red Galliano shirt with dozens of little black ears printed on it, black Armani slacks jingling with loose change, and shoes with tassels on them. His smile was startlingly unappealing.

'How do you do,' said Catherine, playing hostess, though she could tell at a glance that she had no desire to know the answer.

'*Prima, prima,*' exclaimed the composer, bounding into the house with a lightness of step possibly achieved by the feeble claims of gravity on his four-foot-eleven frame. Already bald at twenty-nine, he had a face like a macaque. Even Ben Lamb, who was usually most careful not to gape at people with physical peculiarities, couldn't quite believe what Fate had delivered.

Pino had parked his Porsche as close to the front door as possible without driving it into the house, and, as Signor and Signora Courage strove to make him welcome, he kept glancing through the window, as if worried that some delinquent forest animal was liable to drive off with his splendid vehicle.

Calmed at last, he spread his arms beneficently and invited the music to begin.

The Courage Consort sang *Partitum Mutante* – all thirty-one and a half minutes of it, without a break – and they sang it rather well, all things considered. As always, when it came to the challenge of a real performance to an audience – even an audience of one – they moved Heaven and Hell to overcome their differences. Julian managed nuances of some humility, Dagmar conformed for the greater good, Roger slowed his tempo when his wife faltered at one point, gathering her back into the fold. And, at the finish, Catherine sang the last notes with even greater virtuosity than she had before.

Arboreal silence settled on the house as the Courage Consort slumped, exhausted, on the farther shores beyond conventional harmony. They had swum a long way in turbulent sonic waters with barely a pause for breath. Rather disconcertingly, as they struggled up from the sea, they felt themselves being looked down on by a macaque in an infant's pyjama jacket.

'Bravo,' the macaque leered.

Pino Fugazza was, briefly, lavish in his praise, then, at length, lavish in his criticism. As he spoke, he left the score unconsulted at his side; matters of mere pedantic detail did not seem to trouble him. Instead, it was larger issues that he felt the Consort were failing to grasp. Issues like the very essence and spirit of the piece.

Gesticulating balletically, Fugazza swayed before them, his slacks jingling as he strove to make himself understood in his own avant-garde version of English.

'It shoot be more extrème, but more soft also,' he exclaimed after many abortive attempts. To illustrate some sort of sublime paradox, he threw his stubby claws violently up into the air, then let them float languorously down like dying squidlets. 'Like somesing very lo-o-o-ost, from ze bottom of a well.'

There was a pause.

'Quieter?' Roger attempted to translate.

Fugazza nodded, pleased that progress was being made at last.

'Yes, very much quieter,' he said, 'but wiz no losing of . . . of psychic loudity, you understand?

Quiet, but loud inside ze ears . . . Like ze sound
of water dripping from a . . . a . . .'

'Tap?'

'Faucet. Dripping in ze night, when every-
sing is quiet. So it's loud, yes? Silence,
amplificated.'

They all pondered this a moment, then
Roger said:

'You think we should sing extremely quietly,
but have microphones amplifying us?'

'No! No! No microphones!' cried Pino,
plucking invisible offending objects from the air
in front of him and casting them straight into a
lake of fire. 'Ze loudness comes from ze . . . ze
intensity, yes?'

'Intensity of emotion?'

'Intensity of . . . of concentration. Concentrated like . . . like . . .'

'Chicken stock cubes?' suggested Dagmar in
a poisonous murmur as she played with a strand
of her hair.

'Like a bullet,' affirmed the composer in
triumph. 'A bullet is very small, yes? But ze
effect is . . . is . . .' He grimaced, betrayed yet
again by a language so inferior to Italian.

Catherine, resisting the urge to leave her

body and float up to the ceiling after her big exertion, tried hard to help him find the right word. She imagined the effect of a bullet entering someone's flesh – someone who didn't want to die.

'Dreadful,' she said.

'I hate him,' hissed Dagmar when he had driven away.

'It's probably a communication problem,' said Roger spiritlessly.

'I hate him,' repeated Dagmar, intently flicking her damp hair with her thumb and index finger. 'That's what I'm communicating to you.'

'Well,' sighed Roger, 'he has *his* idea of the piece, we have ours . . .'

Ben was padding around the house like a bear, going from window to window, opening them all wide. It wasn't until he was opening the biggest, nearest window that his fellow Consort members noticed the whole chateau stank of the sort of perfume probably derived from scraping the scrotums of extremely rare vermin.

United in their dislike of the composer, the

Courage Consort devoted the next week to getting on top of *Partitum Mutante*. By day, they did little other than sing. By night, they slept deeply. Even Catherine was less troubled by insomnia than ever before. No sooner had the piercing, plaintive cry of the creature in the forest woken her up than she was drifting off again.

In the Chateau de Luth, she was developing a kind of routine, to which, amazingly for her, she was able to adhere religiously. She who had always seemed programmed to disappoint, abandoning the best-laid late-night plans in the suicidal torpor of dawn, was now getting up early every morning, cooking porridge for Ben, going off for a bike ride with Dagmar, then freshening herself up for a long afternoon's singing. Looking down at herself in the shower as the misty water cascaded over her naked flesh, she wondered if she was merely imagining a more youthful appearance, or if it was real.

Roger was retreating into a hard shell of professionalism, a state he tended to go into whenever a deadline was growing too near. It was by no means unattractive: Catherine liked him best this way. He focused utterly on the task at hand – in this case, the fiendish *Partitum Mutante* – and strove to understand the nature of his fellow singers' difficulties, keen not to dissipate their precious energy or fray their raw nerves. Rather than demanding endless repetition, he was tolerant when things went wrong. 'Let's not waste our breath,' he'd quip gravely, whenever an argument loomed. Afterwards, he'd lie flat on his back in bed at night thinking up ways to make the next performance run more smoothly. Catherine almost felt like embracing him when he was like this. If she could have been sure he'd stay flat on his back, she would have rested her head on his shoulder and stroked his frowning brow.

She wondered if Ben was happy. He was such a mountain of poise, but was he happy? Every night at 11 p.m. sharp, he would retire to his little room, to a bed that could not possibly be big enough for him. What did he do to make himself comfortable? Did he miss his wife? Was his own body, when he was horizontal, intolerably heavy, like an unwanted other person bearing down on him?

Before this fortnight in Martinekerke, it would never have occurred to Catherine to wonder about such things. Each Consort member had his or her separate life, mysterious to the others. Their personal happiness or unhappiness was irrelevant to the purpose that brought them together – at least, that was the way it had always been in the past. They would *rendezvous* at the Lambs' place in Tufnell Park, like five football fans who were going to sit down and watch a televised match together, and with barely a word spoken they would start singing a Josquin *Miserere* or whatever was on the agenda. Ben's wife would make herself scarce, cooking what smelled like very large quantities of Asian food in the kitchen. In all the years the Consort had been doing this, Catherine had never even got around to asking what nationality Mrs Lamb was. She looked Vietnamese or something, and dressed like an American hair-care consultant. At intervals, she would serve her guests coffee and cake: apple and cinnamon slices subtly impregnated with stray aromas of prawns, turmeric, garlic, soy sauce. Now and then Catherine got a hankering to ask Ben a few questions about his wife, but as the years passed she tended to feel she might have missed the right moment to raise the subject.

Julian was an unknown quantity too, although there were signs that he might inspire complex emotions in more people than just his fellow singers. Once, while the Consort were rehearsing at the Lambs' house, a drunken man, shouting unintelligible abuse, had kicked dents into Julian's car parked just outside. Julian went white and sat waiting stoically as the characteristic *bimff* of breaking windscreen resounded in the night air. Again, no one in the Courage Consort asked any questions. Julian's extra-musical activities were his own affair. He could sing the pants off any tenor in England, that was the important thing.

Even Catherine's mental frailties were tolerated, as long as they didn't interfere with the music. Last year, she'd even been able to show up for rehearsals with both her wrists wrapped in snowy white bandage, and nobody had mentioned it. By contrast, if she dared to spend a few minutes too long in Heathrow's toilets when the Consort had a plane to catch, she was liable to hear an admonitory summons over the airport PA.

As for Dagmar, the most recent addition to the group, she'd stuck with the Courage Consort because they gave her fewer hassles than any of her many previous liaisons. After walking out on the Dresden Staatsoper because the directors seemed to think she was too sexually immoral to sing opera (her last rôle for them was Berg's prostitute Lulu, for God's sake!) she'd been a bit wary of these smiling English people, but it had turned out OK. They allowed her to get away with tempestuous love affairs, even illegitimate pregnancy, as long as she showed up on time, and this she had no trouble with. For nine months of ballooning belly she'd never missed a rehearsal; she'd given birth, prudently, during the lull between Ligeti's *Aventures* in Basle and the 'Carols Sacred and Profane' Christmas concert in Huddersfield. That was good enough for Roger Courage, who had sent her a tasteful congratulations card without enquiring after the baby's name or sex.

This strange fortnight in Martinekerke, though, was making them so much more real to each other as human beings, at least from Catherine's point of view. Living together as a family, cooking for each other, seeing the stubble on each other's faces — well, not on hers, of course — watching each other's hair grow, even

. . . Catherine was finding it all really quite exciting. She could definitely see herself, before the fortnight was over, asking Ben about his wife, or cycling all the way to Duidermonde.

It was her impression, though, that Julian was not a happy man. As the days in the Chateau de Luth wore on, he was growing increasingly restless. Not restless in the sense of lacking ability to concentrate on the task at hand; he worked as hard on *Partitum Mutante* as any of the Consort. Nor restless in the sense of itching for physical exercise; he was quite content to let Dagmar and Catherine cycle daily to Martinekerke to fetch their supplies. No, it appeared he was restless sexually.

In London, Julian was a lone wolf, never actually seen with a partner. Roger and Catherine had always assumed he must be gay, what with the Freddie Mercury ansaphone message and the waspish comments he was wont to make, but in Martinekerke it became clear that, at the very least, he was prepared to stoop to females if nothing better was available.

Females were in limited supply in the forest, but Julian made the most of what strayed his way. The first time Gina had come to clean the chateau, Julian behaved (Roger told Catherine later) like a gallant lord of the manor receiving an impressionable guest. The girl's flat refusal to let him carry her equipment frustrated this line of approach and so he hurried back indoors to launch Plan B, leaving the formal introductions to Roger. When, less than two minutes later, the time came for Gina to be introduced to Julian Hind, 'our tenor', he was already seated at the piano, playing a piece of Bartók's *Mikrokosmos* with serene intensity. He turned his cheekbones towards her and raised his eyebrows, as if he'd never glimpsed her before this moment, as if she'd just blundered, childlike, into a *sanctum* whose holiness she couldn't be expected to understand. He inclined his head in benign welcome but did not speak. Disappointingly, Gina did not speak either, preferring to get down to business. With the plug of the vacuum cleaner nestled in her hand, she nosed around the room, murmuring to herself: 'Stopcontact, stopcontact' – the Dutch word for power-point, apparently. Once the vacuum cleaner started its noisy sucking, Julian stopped playing the piano and settled for a more passive role. Then, all too soon, Catherine had returned from her walk in the woods, and it was time for *Partitum Mutante*.

The second time Gina came to the chateau, five days later, Catherine was actually there, privileged to witness the changes that Julian's growing discontentment had wrought on him. It was an extraordinary sight, an unforgettable testament to the power of accumulated sexual craving.

To begin with, he welcomed her at the door as if she were royalty – the English rather than the Dutch kind – and immediately tried to get her to sit down with him on the sofa. When she insisted that she had work to do, he followed her from room to room, raising the volume of his velvety tenor to compete with the noise of motorised suction and clanking, sloshing buckets. He guessed, correctly, that she was involved in the expressive arts and only doing this cleaning work as a way of supplementing a government grant. He guessed, correctly, her birth sign, her taste in music, her favourite drink, her preferred animal. Dashing into the bathroom to fetch her some Elastoplast when she'd cut her finger, he returned naked from the waist up and with water combed through his hair, complaining of the heat.

Catherine didn't dare follow them upstairs, so she made herself a cup of tea, wondering despite herself whether there was going to be some sexual activity in the chateau after all. By the time she saw Julian again, ten minutes later, he was installed on the sofa, fully dressed, glowering into a book. A strange sound — bed-springy, rhythmic – from upstairs was eventually decoded as Gina slamming an iron onto a padded ironing board.

♫♫♫

Four days before the end of the fortnight, Jan van Hoeidonck dropped in to see how they were getting on. Re-acquainting himself with Catherine Courage, he at first thought she must be the sporty German contralto he'd been told about, she was so tanned and healthy-looking. He'd fixed Catherine in his memory as a slightly stooped middle-aged lady dressed in taupe slacks and a waterproof, with a freshly-washed halo of mousy hair; here she was in green leggings and a berry-stained T-shirt, standing tall, her hair shiny, plastered with sweat. She'd just been for a long cycle, she said.

The real German woman appeared moments

later, cradling a sleeping baby in her arms. She shook Jan by the hand, supporting her infant easily in one arm as she did so.

'This is Dagmar Belotte,' said Roger, 'and . . . erm . . . Axel.'

As a way of breaking the ice, Jan made the mistake of asking Dagmar, rather than Roger Courage, what the Consort's impression of Pino Fugazza had been.

'I hate him,' she volunteered. 'He is a nut case and he smells bad.'

'Extraordinary composer, though, of course,' interjected Roger.

'Don't you check them out before you give them money?' said Dagmar.

The director smiled, unfazed. The German girl's frankness made much more sense to him than the strange, twitching discomfiture of the pale Englishman.

'Pino is very crazy, yes,' he conceded. 'Sometimes crazy people make very good music. Sometimes not. We will find out.'

'And if it's bad?' enquired Dagmar.

Jan van Hoeidonck pouted philosophically.

'Bad music is not a problem in our circles,' he said. 'Ten years later, it's completely disappeared. Biodegradable. It's not like pop music. Bad pop music lasts forever. Johann Strauss. Herman's Hermits. Father Abraham and the Smurfs. These things will never die, even if we put a lot of effort into killing them. But for bad serious music, we don't need to do anything. It just sinks into the ground and it's gone.'

'But Jan, what do *you* think of *Partitum Mutante*?' asked Roger.

'I haven't heard it yet.'

'You've seen the score, surely.'

The director gratefully accepted the steaming cup of coffee being handed to him by Mrs Courage.

'I am a facilitator of musical events,' he explained carefully. 'I read budget sheets. There are enough *crescendos* there, I promise you.' His face was solemn as he said this, though there was a twinkle in his eyes.

Dagmar excused herself and the conversation moved on to more general matters, like the chateau and its facilities. Were the Consort enjoying their stay? How was the environment suiting them?

The big fat man called Ben Lamb, sitting in the far corner of the room, made a small gesture indicating no complaints. Roger Courage said something to the effect that concentration on a musical project made the outside world cease to exist, but that during the brief moments when his Consort was not beavering away at *Partitum Mutante*, the Chateau de Luth and its setting were very attractive indeed. Julian Hind deflected the question, preferring to discuss with the director the feasibility of a hire-car from Antwerp or Brussels.

'I was wondering,' Catherine said, when Julian, appalled at the high cost of Netherlandish living, had retreated to his room. 'You've had many artists staying in this chateau over the years, haven't you?'

'Very many,' affirmed the director.

'Have any of them ever mentioned strange noises in the night?'

'What kind of noises?'

'Oh . . . cries from the forest, perhaps.'

'Human cries?'

'Mmm, yes, possibly.'

She and Roger were sitting together on the sofa. On the pretence of bending down to fetch his plate of cake off the floor, Roger knocked his knee sharply against hers.

'Excuse me, dear,' he warned, trying to pull her back from whatever brink she was dawdling towards.

Unexpectedly, however, the director had no difficulty with her claims of mysterious cries in the night; in fact, he went pensive, as if faced with something that genuinely might lie outside the scope of art and arithmetic.

'This is a story I have heard before, yes,' he said. 'In fact, it is a kind of legend about the forest here.'

'Really,' breathed Catherine, gazing at him over the top of her steaming coffee mug. Roger was already fading away next to her.

'It began, I think, at the end of the war. A . . .' Jan van Hoeidonck paused, checking the Dutch–English dictionary in his head. 'A mental defective mother . . . can you say this in English?'

'It's all right,' said Catherine, loath to explain political correctness to a foreigner. 'Go on.'

'A mental defective mother ran away from Martinekerke with her baby, when the army, the liberating army, was coming. She didn't understand these soldiers were not going to kill her. So she ran away, and nobody could find her. For all the years since that time, there are reports that a baby is crying in the forest, or a . . . a spirit, yes?'

'Fascinating,' said Catherine, bending forward to put her cup down on the floor without taking her eyes off Jan van Hoeidonck. His own gaze dropped slightly, and she realised, with some surprise, that he was looking at her breasts.

I'm a woman, she thought.

Roger spoke up, pulling the conversation back towards Pino Fugazza and his place in contemporary European music. Had the director, in fact, heard *anything* by the composer?

'I heard his first major piece,' Jan replied, unenthusiastically. '*Precipice*, for voices and percussion – the one that won the Prix d'Italia. I don't remember it so well, because all the other Prix d'Italia entries were played on the same night, and they also were for voices and percussion. Except one from the former Soviet Union, for flügelhorn and ring modulator . . .'

'Yes, but can you remember *anything* about Fugazza's piece?' pursued Roger.

The director frowned: for him, dwelling on musical events that were in the past rather than the future was obviously quite unnatural.

'I only remember the audience,' he admitted, 'sitting there after four hours of singing and whispering and noises going bang without warning, and finally it's over, and they don't know if it's time to clap, and soon they will go home.'

Roger was getting politely exasperated.

'Well . . . if you haven't heard *Partitum Mutante*, what makes you think it'll be any better?'

Jan waved a handful of fingers loosely around his right temple.

'He has since that time had a big mental breakdown,' he said. 'This could be a very good thing for his music. Also, public interest in Fugazza is very high, which is good for ticket sales. He is very famous in the Italian press for attacking his wife with a stiletto shoe at the baggage reclaim of Milan Airport.'

'No!' said Catherine incredulously. 'Is she all right?'

'She is very fine. Soon I think she will be divorced and very wealthy. But of course, the music must stand or fall on its own qualities.'

'Of course,' sighed Roger.

Later, when the director had left, Roger

stood at the window, watching the yellow minibus dwindling into the distance, on the long black ribbon towards Brussels. As he watched, the sun was beaming through the window-panes like a trillion-watt spotlight, turning his silver hair white and his flesh the colour of peeled apple. Every age line and wrinkle, every tiny scar and pockmark from as far back as adolescence, was lit up in harsh definition. Eventually the intensity of the light grew too much for him; he turned away, fatigued, blinking and wiping his eyes.

Noticing that Ben Lamb was still sitting in the shady corner of the room, and Catherine lying sweating and sleepy on the couch, he allowed himself to express his first pang of doubt about the value of the project they were all engaged on.

'You know, I'm really rather tired of this glamour that madness is supposed to have, aren't you?' he said, addressing Ben. 'It's the little marks on the score that ought to be sensational, not the behaviour of Italian lunatics at airports.'

Catherine, not happy at the disrespect with which madness was being tossed about here, said:

'Couldn't this Pino fellow just be young and excitable? I wouldn't presume to judge if anyone was definitely mad. Especially an Italian I've only met once. He surely can't be *too* barmy if he drives a Porsche and wears Armani.'

'Poetically put, dear – if somewhat mysterious in reasoning,' remarked Roger.

'No, I meant, he's obviously not . . . um . . . otherwordly, is he?'

There was a pause as the men pondered the significance of this word.

'What do *you* think, Ben?' said Roger.

'I think we should sing as much as we possibly can in the next four days,' said Ben, 'so that, by the time of the première, we can at least be sure of being less confused than Mr Fugazza.'

♫

And so they sang, as the sun blazed in the sky and the temperature inside the chateau climbed towards 30° Celsius. It was worse than being under a full rig of stage lights; all five of them were simmering in their clothes.

'We'll end up performing this in the nude,' suggested Julian. 'That'll put some sensuality into it!'

The others let it pass, appreciating that he was a man on heat.

When, at last, they were all too tired to go on, Roger and Julian went to bed – not with each other, of course, though lately Julian looked as if he might soon consider anything, even his fellow Consort members, as a sexual possibility. His initial disgust at seeing Dagmar breast-feed had, with the passing days, softened to tolerance, and then hardened to a curiosity whose keenness embarrassed everyone except himself. Dagmar, usually indifferent to the petty libidos of unwanted men, grew self-conscious, and the feeding of her baby became an increasingly secret act, perpetrated behind closed doors. In Julian's presence, she tended to fold her arms across her breasts, protectively, aggressively. After half an hour staring Julian down, she would leap up and start pacing back and forth, a dark band across her bosom where her sweaty forearms had soaked the fabric of whatever she was wearing.

On the night of the director's visit, with *Partitum Mutante* finished off and Julian safely gone to bed, Dagmar sat slumped on the couch, Axel at her breast. Ben sat by the open window, staring out at a sky which, even at a quarter to eleven, still had some daylight left in it. The unearthly quiet was descending again, so that even the drip of a tap in the kitchen could be heard from the front room.

Oddly revived by having had her milk sucked from her, Dagmar decided to take Axel out for a walk in the forest. She did not invite Catherine; the older woman guessed this must be one of those times when Dagmar wanted to have the run of the world alone with her baby, explaining things to him in German.

'Be careful,' said Catherine as they were leaving. 'Remember the legend.'

'What legend?'

'A mother and her child disappeared in that forest once, at the end of the war. Some people say the baby is still out there.'

Dagmar paused momentarily as she made a mental calculation.

'Well, if we meet a fifty-seven-year-old baby on our walk, maybe Axel will like to play with him,' she said, and sauntered into the dark.

Left alone with Ben, Catherine weighed up the pros and cons of going to bed. On the pro side, she was exhausted. But the house had absorbed so much heat that she doubted she would sleep.

'Do you want anything, Ben?' she offered.

'Mm? No, thanks,' he replied. He was still sitting by the window, his white shirt almost transparent with sweat. For all his bear-like bulk, he had no body hair, as far as Catherine could see.

'How are you, anyway?' she asked. It seemed a faintly absurd question, this late in the night.

'Tired,' he said.

'Me too. Isn't it funny how we've lived here together, day after day, and sung together end-lessly, and yet we hardly say two words to one another?'

'I'm not much of a conversationalist.'

He closed his eyes and leaned his head back, as if about to release his soul into the ether, leaving his body behind.

'You know,' said Catherine, 'after all these years, I know hardly anything about you.'

'Very little to tell.'

'I don't even know for sure what nationality your wife is.'

'Vietnamese.'

'I thought so.'

Their communication eddied apart then, but not disturbingly. The room's emotional acoustic was not full of shame and failure, like the silences between her and Roger. Silence was Ben's natural state, and to fall into it with him was like joining him in his own world, where he was intimately acquainted with each sleeping soundwave, and knew no fear.

After a while, sitting in the golden-brown front room with Ben in the stillness, Catherine glanced at her watch. It was almost midnight. Ben had never stayed up so late before.

'Did you always want to be a singer?' she asked.

'No,' he said. 'I wanted to carry on coxing.'

She laughed despite herself. 'Carry on *what*?' She was reminded of those dreadful comedy films her father had never allowed her to see, even when she was old enough to be going out with Roger Courage.

'At university,' Ben explained, 'I was a coxswain in a rowing team. I called instructions through a loudhailer. I enjoyed that very much.'

'What happened?'

'I became involved in the anti-Vietnam war

movement. Cambridge wasn't the most left-wing place in those days. I lost most of my friends. Then I got fat.'

You're not fat, Catherine wanted to reassure him, as a reflex kindness, then had to struggle to keep a straight face in the moon face of absurdity. Reassurance is such a sad, mad thing, she thought. Deep inside, everyone knows the truth.

'What do you really think of *Partitum Mutante*, Ben?'

'We-e-ell . . . it's a plum part for a bass, I have to admit. But I don't see us singing it far into the twenty-first century somehow.'

Again the silence descended. Minutes pass-ed. Catherine noticed for the first time that there were no clocks in the Chateau de Luth, except for those inside the computers and the oven, and the wrist-watches worn by the human visitors. Perhaps there had once been splendid old timepieces which some previous guest had stolen – she imagined Cathy Berberian stealthily wrapping an antique clock up in her underwear as she was packing her suitcase to go home. Perhaps there had never been clocks on these walls at all, because the chateau's furnishers had understood that the sound of seconds ticking would have been maddening, intolerable, in the forest's silence.

Suddenly, there was a plaintive, inarticulate wail from outside, a cry that was more high-pitched and eerie than anything Axel was capable of. Catherine's flesh was thrilled with fear.

'There!' she said to Ben. 'Did you hear that?'

But, looking across at him, she saw that his eyes were shut, his great chest rising and falling rhythmically.

Catherine jumped up from the couch, hurried to the front door. She opened it – very quietly so as not to wake Ben – and peered out into the night, which was impenetrably dark to her unadjusted eyes. The forest was indistinguishable from the sky, except that there were stars in one and not the other. Catherine was half-convinced that Dagmar and Axel had been consumed by some lonely demon, swallowed up into the earth, never to be seen again. It was almost disappointing when, minutes later, both mother and baby materialised out of the gloom and strolled up to the chateau, Dagmar's white trainers luminescing.

'Did you hear the cry?' said Catherine as Dagmar reached the threshold.

'What cry?' said Dagmar. Axel was wide-eyed and full of energy, but his mother was exhausted, overdue for bed. She swayed in the doorway, looking as if she might consider handing her baby over to Catherine for a while.

♩♩♩♩

Next day, Roger telephoned Pino Fugazza, to tell him that there was a problem with *Partitum Mutante*. A technical problem, he said. They'd rehearsed it so thoroughly now, he said, that they were in a position to tell the difference between awkwardnesses that arose from unfamiliarity with the score, and awkwardnesses that might be . . . well, in the score itself.

While Roger spoke, the other members of the Courage Consort sat nearby, wondering how Pino was going to react, especially as Roger was pushed, *poco a poco*, to be more specific about the nature of the problem – which was that, in a certain spot, Pino's time signatures just didn't add up. The Italian's daring musical arithmetic, a tangled thicket of independent polyrhythms, was supposed to resolve itself by the 404th bar (symbolising the 4004 years from Creation to Christ's birth), so that Roger and Catherine were suddenly singing in perfect unison, joined in the next bar by Julian and Dagmar while Ben kept lowing underneath.

'The thing is,' said Roger into the phone, 'by the 404th bar, the baritone is a beat behind the soprano.'

A harsh chattering sound came through the receiver, indecipherable to the overhearers.

'Well . . .' grimaced Roger, adjusting his glasses to look at the computer screen. 'It's possible I've misunderstood something, but three lots of 9/8 and one lot of 15/16 repeated with a two-beat rest . . . are you with me?'

More chatter.

'Yes. Then, from the A flat, it goes . . . Pardon? Uh . . . Yes, I see it right here in front of me, Mr Fugazza . . . But surely thirteen plus eight is twenty-one?'

The conversation was wound up very quickly after that. Roger replaced the telephone receiver on the handset and turned to his expectant fellow members of the Consort.

'He gives us his blessing,' said Roger, frowning in bemusement, 'to do whatever we want.'

It was a freedom none of them would have predicted.

★

Later that afternoon, while the Courage Consort were taking a break to soothe their throats with fruit juice, a car pulled up to the house. Roger opened the door, and let in a grizzled photographer who looked like a disgraced priest.

'Hello! Courage Consort? Carlo Pignatelli.'

He was Italian, but worked for a Luxembourg newspaper, and he'd been sent to cover the Benelux Contemporary Music Festival. He had already seen publicity material on the Consort, and knew exactly what he wanted.

Dagmar was nursing a glass of apricot juice alone in the front room while the English members of the group hung around the oven trying to make toast. Pignatelli made a bee-line for the German girl, who was wearing black tights and a white cotton blouse.

'You're Dagmar Belotte, right?' He sounded alarmingly as if he'd learned English from watching subtitled cockney soap operas; in truth, he'd just returned to the bosom of the European press after ten alcoholic years in London.

'That's right,' said Dagmar, putting her drink down on the floor. She was going to need both hands for this one, she could tell.

'You're into mountaineering, right?' said Pignatelli, as if getting a few final facts straight after a gruellingly thorough interview.

'That's right,' said Dagmar.

'You wouldn't have any of your gear with you, would you?'

'What for?'

'A picture.'

'A picture of what?'

'A picture of you in mountaineering gear. Ropes.' He indicated with his hairy hands where the ropes would hang on her, fortunately using his own chest rather than hers to demonstrate. 'Axe.' He mimed a small act of violence against an invisible cliff face.

'There are no mountains here,' said Dagmar evenly.

The photographer was willing to compromise. Quickly sizing up the feel of the chateau's interior, his eyes lingering for micro-seconds on the rack of antique recorders, he said:

'Play the flute?'

'No.'

'Mind holding one?'

Dagmar was speechless for a moment, which he took as assent. Surprisingly fleet on his feet, he bounded over to the recorders and selected the biggest. Handing it over to her, he leered encouragingly, then drew his camera from its holster with a practised one-handed motion. Dagmar folded her arms across her breasts, clasping the recorder in one fist like a police baton.

'Could you put it in your mouth maybe?' suggested the photographer.

'Forget it,' said Dagmar, tossing the instrument onto a nearby cushion.

'Is there a grand piano?' rejoined the photographer, quick as a flash. She surely wouldn't object to leaning in and fingering a few strings, canopied by the lid.

'No, it's a . . .' The word Dagmar was looking for refused to translate itself from German. She considered saying 'erect' but decided against it. 'Not grand,' she said, her big eyes narrowing to slits.

Undaunted, the photographer peered outside to gauge the weather. Mercifully, a loud noise started up from somewhere inside the house, a disconsolate human cry that could not be ignored.

'Excuse me,' muttered Dagmar as she strode off to find her baby.

The photographer turned his attention immediately to Catherine.

'Is it true,' he said, picking up Dagmar's half-finished tumbler of juice, 'a soprano can shatter glass?'

♫♫♫♫

That night, when the singing was over, the chateau was even hotter than the night before. Catherine found herself alone in the front room with Julian, everyone else having gone to bed.

Julian was on his hands and knees in front of a bookcase, peering at the spines. He had finished everything he'd brought with him to Belgium, all the thrillers and exposés, and was now in the market for something else. He read no Dutch, so such tomes as *Het Leven en Werk van Cipriano de Rore (1516–1565)* didn't quite hit the spot, but he was fluent in French and – surprisingly, to Catherine – Latin.

'Really? Latin?' she said, as if he'd just revealed a facility for Urdu or Sinhalese.

'I don't know why you're so surprised,' said Julian, his bottom – ass? – arse? – in the air as he studied the titles. 'We sing Latin texts all the time.'

'Yes, but . . .' Catherine cast her mind back to the last time she'd sung in Latin, and was surprised at the ease with which she recalled the words of Gabrieli's 'O Magnum Mysterium'. Something was happening to her brain lately, an unblocking of the channels, a cleaning of the contours. 'We use translations. Or I do, anyway. Roger prints out parallel English and Latin texts for me, and that's how I learn what it all means.'

'I don't need Roger to tell me what it all means,' muttered Julian as he pulled an ancient-looking volume out of the bookcase. It slid smoothly into his hands, without the billow of dust Catherine might have expected – but then, Gina had dusted there only a few days ago.

'I think I'll go for a walk,' said Catherine.

'You do that,' said Julian. He was in a peculiar, intense state, as if he'd passed right through frustration into whatever lay beyond. Sitting cross-legged on the carpet, he was opening the fragile old book in his lap and bending his head towards its creamy pages, his damp black hair swinging down over his forehead. For Catherine, it was all indefinably unnerving, and her instinct was to get away.

Roger would still be awake, though, in the

bed upstairs. Roger, Julian, and the dark forest of Martinekerke: she was stuck between the devil, and the devil, and the deep blue sea.

Catherine set off into the night, with a windcheater loosely draped over her T-shirt, and only a pencil torch to guide her through the dark. She didn't even switch it on, but kept it in the back pocket of her jeans, hoping that her sight would adjust to the starlight, the way the eyes of people like Dagmar evidently did.

Walking across the road, Catherine felt and heard, but could not see, her feet stepping off the smooth tarmac into the leafy perimeter of the forest. She rustled cautiously forward, trusting her body aura to warn her of approaching trees. Overhead, the sky remained black; perhaps the awful humidity meant that it was cloudy.

She removed the torch from her pocket and shone its thin beam onto the ground before her. A small circle of leaves and earth stood out from the darkness like an image on a television screen. It moved as she tilted her wrist, scooting backwards and forwards through the trees, growing paler. After only thirty seconds of use, the batteries of the torch were getting tired already; the feeble power supply just wasn't up to the challenge of a whole forest full of night. She switched it off, and hoped for the best.

You know what you've come here for, don't you? challenged a voice from inside her. She wasn't alarmed: it was her own voice, intimate and patient, not the terrifying stranger who had once commanded her to swallow poison or slice through the flesh of her wrists. It was just a little harmless internal conversation, between Catherine and herself.

No, tell me: what am I here for? she asked in return.

You're waiting for the cry, came the answer.

She walked deeper into the forest, afraid and unrepentant. A breeze whispered through the trees, merciful after the trapped and stagnant heat inside the house. She was just getting a breath of fresh air, that was all. There was no such thing as ghosts: a ghost would always be revealed, in the clear light of day, to have been an owl, or a wolf, or one's own father standing in the door of one's bedroom, or a plastic bag caught on a branch, waving in the wind. The dead stayed dead. The living had to push on, without help or hindrance from the spirit world.

Catherine's eyes had adjusted to the dark by now, and she could see the boughs of the trees around her, and an impression of the ground beneath her feet. Wary of getting herself lost but wanting to stay in the forest longer, she wandered in circles, keeping the distant golden lights of the house in sight. She clapped her palms against trees as she passed them, swinging around like a child on a pole. The roughness of the bark was heavenly on her hands.

After perhaps half an hour she grew conscious of a full bladder – all those glasses of fruit juice! – and squatted in a clearing to pee. Her urine rustled into the leaves, and something unidentifiable scratched softly against her naked bottom.

I hope nothing jumps into me while I'm exposed like this, she thought, as, in the chateau, the lights went out.

Next morning, Ben Lamb, waiting for his *havermout*, looked up expectantly as someone entered the kitchen. But it was only Julian, come for his coffee.

'I made a real find last night,' Julian said, as the kettle hissed sluggishly.

'Mm?' said Ben.

'An original edition of Massenet's songs, printed in 1897, including some I'm sure have never seen the light of day, just sitting there on the shelf. Never been looked at!'

'How do you know it's never been looked at?'

'The pages were still uncut. Just think! Totally . . . virgin.'

'And did you cut them, Julian?'

'You bet I did,' grinned Julian. 'And it was a delicious sensation, I can assure you.' He was peering into the refrigerator as Dagmar, fully dressed and with Axel already in her rucksack, passed by the kitchen.

'Save a few eggs for other people, please,' she called over her shoulder.

Julian contorted his face into a gargoyle sneer, beaming malice in her direction as the front door slammed shut.

'*Jawohl, mein Kommandant!*'

Ben sighed. The Courage Consort were reaching the limit of their ability to coexist harmoniously, at least in such hothouse conditions.

It was only 10.30 am now, and the temperature was already stifling; not the best conditions for negotiating the treacherous vocal labyrinths laid out for them by Mr Fugazza. According to an imported *Times* Dagmar had brought back from Martinekerke yesterday, rain was pelting down all over London and the Home Counties: when would the clouds break here?

Roger walked into the kitchen, a veteran of yet another telephone call.

'Wim Waafels, the video artist, is coming here this afternoon,' he said, looking glum.

'Some problem?' enquired Ben.

Roger ran his fingers through his hair, large patches of sweat already darkening the under-arms of his shirt, as he searched for a way to summarise his misgivings.

'Let's just say I don't imagine Dagmar is going to like him very much,' he said at last.

'Oooh,' camped Julian, 'fancy that! A soulmate for me. You never know your luck in a big forest.'

Roger shambled over to the stove, tired of holding his little family together, day after day. He poured himself a cup of tea from the kettle that had boiled, unnoticed.

'Has anyone seen our soprano?' he said, trying to keep his voice light.

Ben shook his head. Julian stared directly into Roger's face, and saw there a look he had a special facility for recognising: the look of a man who is wondering where his wife slept last night.

'She went walkabout,' said Julian. 'After the witching hour.'

Roger sipped at his tea, not a happy man.

Then, a few minutes later, the front door clattered open and footsteps sounded in the hallway. Julian's jaw hardened in anticipation of another German invasion.

Instead, Catherine walked into the kitchen. She walked slowly, dreamily, in no hurry to focus on the men. Her hair was a bird's nest of tangles, her skin was flushed, her eyes half closed. Tiny leaves and fragments of twig clung to the calves of her leggings.

'Are you all right, Kate?' said Roger.

Catherine blinked, acknowledging his existence by degrees.

'Yes, yes, of course,' she responded airily. 'I've been out walking, that's all.'

She padded over to the stove, patting her

husband's shoulder as she passed because the poor thing looked so miserable.

'Would anyone like some porridge?' she said, finding Ben's face exactly where she expected it to be and contemplating it with a smile.

Though there were two hours to kill before Wim Waafels was due to arrive, the Consort did not sing. By unspoken mutual agreement, they were giving *Partitum Mutante* a rest while the weather did its worst. Ben sat by the window, nursing a headache and indigestion; the others mooched around the house, fiddling with the musical instruments, books and ornaments. Julian played Beethoven's 'Für Elise' on the piano, over and over, always getting stuck in the same spot; Catherine squatted at the spinning wheel, touching its various parts tentatively, trying to decide if it was meant to be functional or was just for show. Roger sat at the computer, browsing through the score of Paco Barrios's *2K+5*, reminding himself that there would be life after *Partitum Mutante*.

By the time Mr Waafels ought to be arriving, the British members of the Courage Consort had – again by unspoken mutual consent – pulled together, resolved to be philosophical in the face of whatever the visit might bring. Only Dagmar was exempt from the prevailing mood. She sensed something in Roger's manner which made her suspect that the over-extended strings of her tolerance were about to be twanged.

'You've talked to this man, have you?' she queried warily.

'On the phone, yes,' said Roger.

'Is he a nut case?'

'No, no . . .' Roger reassured her breezily. 'He sounds quite . . . focused, really.'

'So he is OK?'

'He . . . he has a very thick Dutch accent. Much thicker than Jan van Hoeidonck's, for example. He's very young, I gather. *Your* age, perhaps. Not an old fuddy-duddy like us, heh heh heh.'

Dagmar's eyes narrowed in contempt. She'd always had a lot of respect for Roger Courage, but right now he was reminding her of the directors at the Dresden Staatsoper.

A vehicle could be heard approaching the Chateau de Luth, though it was half a mile away yet, invisible.

'That'll be him now,' said Roger, smoothly making his escape from Dagmar to take up a position at the window. But when the vehicle came into view, it proved to be not a van or a car, but a motorcycle, roaring through the stillness of Martinekerke forest in a haze of benzine, its rider in grey leather, studded gloves and a silver helmet, like a medieval soldier come looking for Thierry la Fronde and his band of merry men.

Once they invited him in, Wim Waafels proved to be, physically at least, a slightly more impressive specimen than Pino Fugazza; he could hardly fail to be. Then again, as he was taking off his helmet and leather jacket in the chateau's front room, he did cause several members of the Courage Consort to meditate privately on the infinite scope of human unattractiveness.

He was a young man – twenty-five, reportedly, though he looked seventeen, with an overweight teenager's awkward posture. He wore ochre-coloured cords, military boots and a large threadbare T-shirt on which was printed a much-enlarged still from Buñuel's *Un Chien Andalou* – the razor blade hovering above the woman's eye. Waafels's own eyes were bloodshot and deep-set, full of sincere but rather spe-cialised intelligence. Perspiration and the odd pimple glittered on his pumpkin face; his head was topped with a bush of bleached white hair corrugated with gel.

'Erm . . . is it hotter or cooler, driving here on a motorcycle?' asked Catherine, struggling to make conversation as she handed him a tall drink of orange juice.

'Bose,' he replied.

Though Wim's English vocabulary was good, his accent was so thick that he seemed to have been schooled by a different process from that used by all the other Dutch people they'd met – interactive CD roms, maybe, or those little translator gadgets you saw in brochures that fell out of the *Radio Times*.

More worrying than his accent was the way he blushed and stammered when introduced to Dagmar: evidently he had a weakness for big-breasted young German women with muscular limbs, even if they did not look overly friendly. Perhaps he mistook Dagmar's glower for the mock-dangerous pout of an MTV babe.

'Hi. I'm Wim,' he told her.

'Great. Let's see the video,' said Dagmar.

Small talk having reached its apex, they all got promptly down to business. Wim had brought with him a video of his images for *Partitum Mutante*. On the spine of the cassette, in silver felt-tip, he had scrawled 'PArTiTEm M!' This, more even than Mr Waafels's appearance, caused alarm bells to toll inside the overheated skulls of the Courage Consort.

There was a slight delay as the television proved not to be connected to the video player. To Wim, this was an eyebrow-raising oddity, something that could only be explained in terms of the Courage Consort having fiddled with the leads and plugs while using digital samplers, MIDI keyboards or other sophisticated technologies. He could not have guessed that the Courage Consort simply did not watch television.

Wim Waafels connected the machines with a practised, casual motion, the closest he came to physical grace. He then asked for the curtains to be drawn so the daylight wouldn't interfere with the clarity of his images. Roger obliged, or attempted to.

'Ken it not be moor dark den dis?' Waafels enquired uneasily, as the room glowed amber in the muffled sunlight.

Roger fiddled with the curtains, trying out one thing and another.

'That's as dark as we're going to get it,' he said.

They all kneeled around the television, except for Ben, whose massive body did not permit him to kneel; he sat on the divan, insisting he could see perfectly well from a little farther back.

'OK,' announced Wim. 'De oddience is here, you are on de staitch, de lights go out – blekness!'

The tape started to whirr through the machine, and the screen, at first snowy, went perfectly black. It remained perfectly black for what felt like a very long time, though it was probably only thirty seconds – a minute, at most.

'You heff to imegine you are singing, of coorse,' Wim Waafels counselled them.

'Of course,' said Julian, moving a little closer to the television so that he couldn't see Dagmar's face.

The blackness of the screen was finally softening at its core, to a reddish-purple – or maybe it was an optical illusion brought on by eyestrain. But no: there was definitely something taking shape there.

'In de beginning, de ooniverse woss widout form, yes?' explained Waafels. 'Darkness moofs on de face of de deep.' The videotape as it passed along the machine's play heads made a faint squeaking noise which set Catherine's teeth on edge; she wished Ben could be making his sonorous Tibetan moans to give this gloomy void a human soundtrack.

After an eternity, the inky amorphous swirls finally coalesced into . . . into what? Some sort of glistening mauve orifice.

'Now, do you know what iss it?' challenged Waafels.

There was an awkward pause, then Ben spoke up.

'I believe I do,' he said, his voice calm and gently resonant. 'It's a close-up of a larynx, as seen by a laryngoscope.'

'Ferry goot, ferry goot!' said Waafels, happy to have found a soul on his wavelength. 'In de beginning woss de word, yes? De word dat coms from widdin de focal cords of Got.'

Another eternity passed as the larynx trembled open and shut, open and shut, twinkling in its own juices. Catherine felt queasiness accumulate in her stomach as the picture became lighter and pinker, and she glanced sideways at her companions, to see if they were feeling it too. Roger's face was rigid with concentration, loath to miss any crucial details if and when they should come. Julian and Dagmar, though they would probably have hated to be told so, looked strikingly similar: incredulous, open-mouthed, beautiful in their disdain. Catherine longed to turn and look at Ben, but she didn't want to embarrass him, so she reapplied her attention to the yawning aperture of flesh on the screen. Some sort of digital magic was being employed now to morph the larynx; the labia-like *plica vocalis* and *vallecula* were evolving, cell by cell, into the vulva of a heavily pregnant woman. Then, with agonising slowness, silent minute upon silent minute, the vagina dilated to reveal the slick grey head of a baby.

The Courage Consort spoke not a word as the *largo*-speed birth took its vivid and glistening course on the screen before them. They were all intimately aware, though, that the duration of *Partitum Mutante* was a shade over half an hour, and the timer on the video player kept track of every second.

When, at long last, the newborn Adam or Planet Earth or whatever he was supposed to be was squirming out into existence, his slow-motion slither almost unbearably eventful after what had gone before, the Courage Consort began to breathe again. Soon, they knew, the lights would go on.

'Of coorsc,' said Wim Waafels by way of qualification, 'it's a total different effect like dis, on only a smol screen.'

'I'm sure it is,' said Roger.

'In de life performance, de immitch will be ferry ferry bik, and you will be ferry smol. It will . . . enfelope you.'

'Mmm,' said Roger, as he might have done if a Bedouin chieftain was watching him eat sheep's eyes at a politically delicate banquet.

'Mmm,' agreed Catherine, suddenly glad to have her husband around to suggest *le mot juste*.

Then, with heavenly timing, little Axel started crying upstairs, and Dagmar's ascension from the room was a *fait accompli* before Wim Waafels had a chance to ask her what she thought. He looked a little crestfallen to have lost the only member of his generation so abruptly, but he turned to the older, less gorgeous members of the Consort without ill feeling.

'Dis giffs you an idea, I hope?' he said to Julian, plainly the next-closest to him in age.

'It does, it does,' said Julian archly. 'I'm sure no one who sees this extraordinary work of yours will ever be able to forget it. My only regret is that I shall be on stage rather than in the audience.'

Waafels hastened to reassure him that this base was covered.

'I will make a video,' he said, 'off de performance.'

'Splendid! Splendid!' crowed Julian, turning away from Roger Courage so as not to be inhibited by the older man's warning stare. 'A video within a video. How very postmodern!'

Waafels smiled shyly as the grinning Julian slapped him on the back.

Later, when Wim Waafels had gone home and Julian had excused himself, the Courages turned to Ben, who was pensively examining the first couple of printed pages of *Partitum Mutante*'s score.

'Well, what do you think, Ben?' sighed Roger.

'I'm too old to claim to know anything about video art,' Ben conceded graciously. 'There is one little thing that worries me, though.'

Still a bit pale and peakish from the slow-motion gush of afterbirth, Catherine waited in silence for him to give voice to his concern.

'While it's utterly dark, in the blackness before the world is born,' mused Ben, 'how are we to see the music?'

The following day was the Consort's second-last in the Chateau de Luth, and they spent most of it arguing.

Things started off civilly enough, in the short-lived morning hours of freshness before the heat set in. Catherine made Ben his *haver-mout* breakfast as usual, serene with pleasure at this wordless routine of nurture. He ate, she watched, as the sun flowed in on both of them, making them glow like lightbulbs. When it got too bright for comfort, Catherine squinted but did not stop looking, and Ben kept his eyes lowered, smiling into the steam of his porridge.

Julian was holed up in his room, no doubt to avoid a reprise of last night's unpleasantness with Roger over the Waafels affair. Roger had disapproved of Julian's sarcasm on the grounds that Waafels, if he'd taken it to heart, would have regarded Julian as speaking for the Courage Consort as a whole; Julian retorted that he damn well hoped he *was* speaking for the Courage Consort as a whole and that if Roger had any deep-seated enthusiasm for singing inside a pair of labia the size of a barn door he'd better come clean with it immediately.

In the wake of this altercation, there'd been a curious change to the chateau's atmosphere, sonically speaking. Julian had removed the television from the public domain and carried it upstairs in his arms, claiming that if he was going to endure another sleepless night he needed something to keep him from going gaga. And, indeed, by midnight Catherine was hearing, from her own bed, the muted sounds of argument and tender Dutch reconciliation coming through the wall. It was a change from the uncanny silence, but not necessarily a welcome one.

This morning, although she couldn't hear

any identifiable television sounds filtering down into the kitchen, Catherine had a feeling it was probably still chattering away to Julian in his room, because the purity seemed to have been taken out of the silence somehow. There was an inaudible fuzz, like the sonic equivalent of haze from burning toast, obscuring Catherine's access to the acoustic immensity of the forest. She would have to go out there soon, and leave that haze behind.

Inconveniently, Dagmar didn't want to go for a cycle. Looking fed up and underslept, she came into the kitchen with no discernible purpose except to check that Julian hadn't touched the eggs in the fridge.

'My nipples are cracking up,' she grouched, causing Ben to blush crimson over his *havermout* behind her. 'First, one was still OK, now it's both of them. Today, it must rain – must, must, must. And I don't understand why you people let that asshole Wim Waafels go without hurting him.'

Having run out of non sequiturs, she slammed the door of the refrigerator and tramped out of the kitchen.

Catherine and Ben sat in silence as they

heard Dagmar ambush Roger in the next room and start an argument with him. The German girl's voice came through loud and clear, an angry contralto of penetrating musicality. Roger's baritone was more muted, his words of pained defence losing some of their clarity as they passed through the walls.

'There was never any suggestion,' he was saying, 'that we had any choice . . .'

'I'm a singer,' Dagmar reminded him. 'Not a doll for nut cases to play with.'

Roger's voice droned reasonably: '. . . multi-media event . . . we are only one of those media . . . problem with all collaborations . . . compromise . . . I'm not a Catholic, but I sing settings of the Latin Mass . . .'

'This is the Dresden Staatsoper all over again!'

On and on they went, until the listeners ceased to take in the words. Instead, Catherine and Ben let the sound of the arguers' voices wallow in the background, an avant-garde farrago of *Sprechstimme*.

By and by, Julian came downstairs and, smelling blood, gave mere coffee and toast a miss and joined the fray instead.

This was too much for Roger: fearing unfair odds, he called a meeting of the Consort as a whole, and the five of them sat in the front room where they had sung *Partitum Mutante* so endlessly, and bickered.

'The way to stop this sort of fiasco ever happening again,' declared Julian, 'is to price ourselves right out of the loony market.'

'What on earth do you mean by that, Julian?' sighed Roger.

'Sing much more popular repertoire and command higher ticket prices. Do more recordings, get our pretty faces known far and wide. Then, whenever we're offered a commission, we pick and choose. And keep some sort of right of veto. No Italian arms dealers, no gynaecology buffs.'

'But,' Roger winced, 'hasn't our strength always lain in our courage? – that is, our . . . um . . . willingness to be open to new things?'

Catherine started giggling, thinking of the yawning vulva that was waiting to 'enfelope' them all.

'Perhaps Kate is, in her own way, reminding us of the need for a sense of humour,' Roger suggested rather desperately.

'No, no, I was just . . . never mind,' said Catherine, still chortling into the back of her hand. Roger was staring at her mistrustfully, imploringly: she knew very well he was trying to decide how crazy she was at this moment, how badly she might let him down. He needed her to be on his side, mentally frail or not; he needed her to see things his way, however impishly her inner demons might prevent her articulating it sensibly. She didn't have the heart to tell him that there weren't any inner demons making her laugh anymore; she just had more important things on her mind right now than the Courage Consort.

'The King's Singers went across a bomb at the Proms,' persisted Julian.

Roger bridled at this; it was a sore point with him. 'Look, I didn't cast my boat out on the dangerous sea of *a cappella* music,' he remarked testily, 'to sing "Obla-di, Obla-da" to a crowd of philistines in funny hats.'

'A very *large* crowd,' Julian reminded him. 'How many people are going to be hearing us at the Benelux Contemporary Music Festival?'

'For God's sake, Julian, are you suggesting we sing Andrew Lloyd Webber and "Raindrops

Keep Falling on My Head" in motet style?'

'Oh bravo, Mr Courage: *reductio ad absurdum*!' Julian was rearing up alarmingly, balletic with pique. 'I'm merely hummmmmbly suggesting you give a *thought* to what might put some reasonably intelligent *bums* on seats. The Beatles, it may *astound* you to know, inspire greater love than Pino Fugazza and Mr Waffle put together – if such a pairing can be imagined without an ejaculation' – he gasped for breath – 'of vomit.'

'Yes, but . . .'

'You know what would make a great encore for us?' raged Julian, quite crazed by now. 'Queen's "Bohemian Rhapsody", arranged for five voices.'

Dagmar snorted loudly.

'You think I'm joking?' exclaimed Julian, fizzing with mischief. 'Listen!' And he burst into song, a snatch of "Bohemian Rhapsody" showing off his own range from horrible *faux*-bass to fiercely accurate falsetto: 'Bis-mil-lah! No-o-o-o! We will not let you go – Let him go-o-o-o! Will not let you go – Let him go-o-o-o! No, no, no, no, no, no, no – Mama mia, mama mia, mama mia let me go . . .'

Mercifully, Julian's fury dissipated before he

reached the 'Beelzebub has a devil put aside' section so familiar from his answering machine, and he slumped back onto his knees.

'You are insane,' pronounced Dagmar, awed, as silence settled again on the sweltering room.

'What do *you* think, Ben?' pleaded Roger.

Ben breathed deeply, blinking as bad vibes continued to float through the thick air.

'I think one thing is not in question,' he said. 'We've been contracted to sing *Partitum Mutante* at the Benelux Contemporary Music Festival. If we do it, some people may question our judgement. If we refuse to do it, many more people will question our professionalism.'

Dagmar shook a heavy lock of hair off her face in a paroxysm of annoyance.

'You are all so British,' she complained. 'You would kill yourself so the funeral company wouldn't be disappointed. Why can't we tell the Benelux Music Festival to shove their Fugazzas and Waafels up their ass?'

'Aahh . . . Perhaps we should approach this from the other end, so to speak,' said Roger, with grim optimism. 'We all seem to be assuming that the fall-out from this event is going to be bad for our reputation – but who's to say it won't be the best thing that ever happened to us? If *Partitum Mutante* outrages everybody and gets the press steamed up, that'll generate a lot of word of mouth about the Consort. In that sense, whatever we may feel in our heart of hearts, the whole affair may push us up to another level of recognition.'

'Oh, you slut, Roger,' said Julian with a sarky pout.

'I *beg* your pardon?'

'I meant it good-naturedly.'

Plainly, the discussion was doomed to be all down-hill from here, but unfortunately there were still many hours of the day to get through. On and on, inexorable as a body function, the argument spasmed blindly along. Catherine, though she was kneeling in the midst of the battle, watched it as if from a distance. She knew Roger wouldn't ask her opinion, not after she'd giggled; he'd be too afraid she'd disgrace him by chattering about underpants. Or he might be worried she'd just stare back at him in a soulless daze, as though he'd tried to summon her from the bottom of a deep, deep well. He didn't realise she was elsewhere now.

It didn't impress her, actually, all this bluster

about *Partitum Mutante* and the Consort's future, and she took pleasure in the fact that it didn't impress Ben either. As often as she could get away with it, short of embarrassing them both, she turned to look at him and smiled. He smiled back, pale with tiredness, while between him and Catherine the stinging voices ricocheted.

She thought: *Dare I do something that might lead to the end of two marriages?*

In the end, it was Axel who came to the rescue again. Strange how this unmusical little creature, this uninvited marsupial whom they'd all imagined would meddle constantly with the serious business of singing, had left them to commune with *Partitum Mutante* uninterrupted for two solid weeks, only making himself heard when he could exercise his preferred role as peace broker.

Today, he'd allowed the Consort to argue the morning and afternoon away, content at first to impose no more ambitious restrictions than to remind them, every few hours, to take a short break for food and drink. However, when nighttime came and they were still hard at it, Axel decided that drastic intervention was needed.

Screaming at the top of his lungs, his mission was to lure his mother to his feverish little body, which he'd marinated in sufficient puke and ordure to earn himself a bath. Dagmar, interrupted just as she was about to announce her defection from the Anglo-German alliance, swallowed her words, stomped upstairs – and did not return.

With her departure, some séance-like bond of hostility was broken, and the Courage Consort dispersed, exhausted. They had resolved nothing, and the rain still hadn't come. Julian slunk off to be comforted by the murmurings of Dutch television; Roger said he was going to bed, though the expression of wounded stoicism on his face suggested he might be going to the Mount of Olives to pray.

Catherine and Ben sat in the rehearsal room, alone. Through the windows, the trees of the forest were furry black against the indigo of the night sky.

After a time, Catherine said:

'What are you thinking, Ben?'

And he replied:

'Time is short. It would have been better if we'd done some singing.'

Catherine nestled her cheek inside her folded arms, her arms on the back of the couch. From this angle, only one of her eyes could see Ben; it was enough.

'Sing me a song, Ben,' she murmured.

With some effort he raised himself from his chair, and walked over to a glass cabinet. He swung open its doors and fetched out an ancient musical instrument – a theorbo, perhaps. Some sort of lute, anyway, creaking with its own old-ness, dark as molasses.

Ben returned to his chair, sat down, and found the least absurd place to rest the bulbous instrument on his bulbous body. Then, gently, he began to strum the strings. From deep inside his chest, sonorous as a saxhorn, came the melancholy lyrics of Tobias Hume, *circa* 1645.

> *Alas, poore men*
> *Why strive you to live long?*
> *To have more time and space*
> *To suffer wrong?*

Looking back at a lifetime devoted to warfare and music, dear old Tobias might well have left it at that, but there were many more verses; the music demanded to go on even if there was little to add to the sentiments. Ben Lamb sang the whole song, about nine minutes altogether, strumming its sombre minimalist accompaniment all the while. Then, when he had finished, he got up and carefully replaced the lute in its display case. Catherine knew he was going to bed now.

'Thank you, Ben,' she said, her lips breathing against her forearm. 'Goodnight.'

'Good night,' he said, carrying his body away with him.

An hour later, Roger and Catherine made love. It seemed the only way to break the tension. He reached out for her, his strange and unreachable wife, and she allowed herself to be taken.

'I don't know anymore, I don't know anymore,' he moaned, lonely as she stroked his damp back.

'Nobody knows, darling,' she murmured abstractedly, smoothing his hair with her hands. 'Go to sleep.'

As soon as he had drifted off, she uncovered herself, imagining she was glowing like an ember in the heat. The house was perfectly quiet; Julian's relationship with the television must have run its course. Outside in the forest, the smell of impending rain dawdled over the tree-tops, teasing.

At the threshold of sleep, she thought she was already dreaming; there were disturbing sounds which seemed to be inside her body, the sounds of a creature in distress, struggling to breathe, vibrating her tissues. Then suddenly she was roused by a very real cry from outside herself. A child's cry, frightened and inarticulate. She was pretty sure it was Axel's, but some instinct told her that it was being provoked by something Dagmar couldn't handle alone.

Roger was dead to the world; she left him sleeping as she threw on her dressing-gown and hurried out of the room.

'*Hilfe*!' called Dagmar breathlessly.

Catherine ran into the German girl's room, but Axel was in there alone, squirming and bawling on a bed whose covers had been flung aside.

'Help!'

Catherine rushed into the room next door, Ben's room. Ben was sprawled on the floor next to his narrow bed, his pyjamas torn open to expose his huge pale torso. Dagmar was hunched over him, apparently kissing him on the mouth. Then, drawing back, she laid her hands on his blubberous chest, clasping one brown palm over the other; with savage force she slammed the weight of her shoulders down through her sinewy arms, squashing a hollow into Ben's flesh.

'Airway. Take over,' she panted urgently, as she heaved herself repeatedly onto where she trusted the well-hidden sternum to be. Ben's mountainous chest was so high off the floor that with every heave her knees were lifting into the air.

Catherine leapt across the room and knelt at Ben's head.

'Roger! Julian!' she screamed, then pressed her lips directly over Ben's. In the pauses between Dagmar's rhythmic shoves, she blew for all she was worth. Filling her lungs so deep that they stabbed her, she blew and blew and blew again.

Please, please breathe, she thought, but Ben did not breathe.

Julian burst into the room, and was momentarily overwhelmed by the sight of the two women, Dagmar stark naked and Catherine in a loose gown, kneeling on the floor with Ben.

'Eh . . .' he choked, eyes popping, before the reality dawned on him. He flew out of the room, bellowing, in pursuit of a telephone in the dark.

The light in the Chateau de Luth was dim and pearly on the day that the Courage Consort were due to go home. The weather had broken at last. Baggage cluttered the front room like ugly modern sculpture forcibly integrated with the archaic spinning-wheels, recorders, leather-bound books, lutes.

Jan van Hoeidonck would be arriving any minute now, in his banana-yellow minibus, and then, no doubt, after the house was safely vacated, Gina would come to clean it. A couple of items in the hallway had been badly damaged by the ambulance people as they'd pulled Ben's body out of the narrow aperture, but the owners of the chateau would just have to be understanding, that was all. Antiques couldn't be expected to last forever; sooner or later, the wear and tear of passing centuries would get to them.

Standing at the window, blindly watching the millions of tiny hail-stones swirling and clattering against the panes, Roger at last raised the subject that must be addressed.

'We have to decide what we're going to do,' he said quietly.

Dagmar turned her face away from him, looking down instead at her baby, cradled tight in her arms. She had a pretty good idea what she was going to do, but now was not the time to tell Roger Courage about it.

'The festival isn't yet,' she said, rocking on Catherine's absurdly big plastic suitcase.

'I know, but it's not going to go away either,' said Roger.

'Give it a rest, Roger,' advised Julian softly, hunched over the piano, stroking his long fingers over all the keys without striking any.

Roger grimaced in shame at what he was about to say, what he could not help saying, what he was obliged by his own personal God to say.

'We could manage it, you know,' he told them. 'The bass part of *Partitum Mutante* is the most straightforward, by a long shot. I know a man called Arthur Falkirk, an old friend of Ben's. They sang together at Cambridge . . .'

'No, Roger.'

It was Catherine speaking. Her face was red and puffy, unrecognisable from crying. Before she'd finally calmed down this morning, she had wept more passionately, more uninhibitedly, than she'd done since she was seven. And, as she'd howled, the torrent of rain had dampened the acoustic of the Chateau de Luth, allowing her lament to take its place alongside the creaking of ancient foundations, the clatter of water from drainpipes and guttering, the burring of telephones. Her voice was hoarse now, so low that no one would ever have guessed she sang soprano.

Roger coughed uneasily.

'Ben was very conscientious,' he said. 'He would've wanted . . .'

'No, Roger,' repeated Catherine.

The telephone rang, and she picked up the receiver before her husband could move a muscle.

'Yes,' she croaked into the mouthpiece. 'Yes, the Courage Consort. This is Catherine Courage speaking. Yes, I understand, don't be sorry. No, of course we won't be performing *Partitum Mutante*. Perhaps Mr Fugazza can find another ensemble. A recording might be a more practical option at this late stage, but I'm sure Mr Fugazza can make up his own mind . . . A dedication? That's very kind of you, but I'm not sure if Ben would have wanted that. Leave it with me, let me think about it. Call me on the London number. But not for a few days, if you would. Yes. Not at all. 'Bye.'

Roger stood at the window, his back turned. His hands were clasped behind his back, one limp inside the other. Against the shimmering shower of hail he was almost a silhouette. Outside, a car door slammed; the others hadn't even heard Jan van Hoeidonck's minibus arrive, but it was here now.

Catherine sat next to Dagmar on the suitcase; it was so uselessly big that there was ample space on its rim for both of them.

'Thanks for travelling with us this time,' she whispered in the German girl's ear.

'It's OK,' stated Dagmar flatly. Tears fell from her cheeks onto her baby's chest as she allowed Catherine to clasp one of her hands, those steely young hands that had proved unequal to the challenge of punching the life back into Ben Lamb's flesh.

The sound of a rain-swollen front door being shouldered open intruded on the moment. A great gust of wet, fragrant, earthy air swept into the house, as Jan van Hoeidonck let himself in. Without speaking, he walked into the front room, seized hold of two suitcases – Roger's and

Ben's — and began to lug them out the door. Dagmar and Catherine slipped off Catherine's suitcase and allowed Roger to trundle it away, though it might just as well have been left behind. It was full of clothes she hadn't worn, and food she hadn't eaten. She would travel lighter in future, if there was a future.

Oh Christ, don't start that again, she thought. *Just get on with it.* And she hurried out into the pelting rain.

The yellow minibus was roomier than she remembered, even though, with the addition of Dagmar and Axel, there were more passengers than there'd been last time — in number, if not in mass. Roger sat next to Jan van Hoeidonck as before. The director pulled away from the Chateau de Luth, tight-lipped, concentrating on the view through the labouring wind-screen wipers; the chances that he and Roger would take up the threads of their discussion on the future of the Amsterdam Concertge-bouw seemed slim. Julian sat at the back of the bus, gazing at the cottage as it dwindled into perspective, a picture postcard again, misty behind the deluge.

They had not been driving five minutes when the sky abruptly ran out of rain, and the forest materialised into view as if out of a haze of static. Then, dazzlingly, the sun came out.

Radiating through the tinted glass of the minibus window, the warmth bathed Catherine's face, soothing her cheeks, stinging the raw rims of her eyelids. With the rain gone, the world's acoustic was changing again: the gentle thrum of the engine surfaced from below, and birds began to twitter all around, while inside the bus, the silence of Ben's absence accumulated like stale breath. It was awful, deadly.

Instinctively, to fill the void, Catherine began to sing: the simplest, most comforting little song she knew, an ancient round she had sung before she'd even been old enough to learn its meaning.

Sumer is icumen in
Loude sing cuckoo,
Groweth seed and bloweth mead,
And spring'th the woode now.
Sing cuckoo . . .

Catherine's soprano came out of her hoarse throat shaky and soft, barely in tune. She stared out of the window, not caring what the others thought of her; they could brand her as a nut case if they needed to. The terrible silence was receding, that was the main thing.

Beginning the second verse, she was bewildered to find herself being joined by Julian, a delicate tenor counterpoint offering its assistance to her faltering lead.

Ewe bleateth after lamb,
Low'th after calfe cow,
Bullock sterteth,
Bucke verteth,
Merry sing cuckoo.

Roger had joined in by now, and Dagmar, though she didn't know the words, improvised a strange but fitting descant *sans paroles*.

Cuckoo cuckoo
Well singst thou cuckoo,
Ne swicke thou never now.

Sing cuckoo now,
Sing cuckoo,
Sing cuckoo,
Sing cuckoo now . . .

On and on they sang, not looking at each other, heading home.

MICHEL FABER wrote fiction for twenty-five years before trying to get published. His novel *Under The Skin* (2000), which garnered accolades from around the world, was nominated for the Whitbread and Impac awards. His prize-winning short stories were collected together in *Some Rain Must Fall* (1998). Other books include *The Hundred and Ninety-Nine Steps* (2001) and *The Crimson Petal and the White* (2002). Faber's work is being translated into twenty-nine languages. A Dutch citizen, he was brought up in Australia and has lived in the Scottish Highlands for eleven years.

Praise for Michel Faber's *The Courage Consort*

"The novel is fluent, light and direct . . . Concise and readable, [it] leaves a strange, melancholy aftertaste." *Daily Telegraph*

"Very subtle and completely engaging." Brian Eno

"A devastating portrayal of a woman on the verge of madness . . . His writing is as spare and sharp as ever." *Daily Mail*

"Strangely moving . . ." *Evening Standard*

"Faber's style is elegant and dryly amusing." *The Big Issue in the North*

"Achieving a sophisticated climax, Faber's depiction of the mental and emotional workings of the quintet is perfect." *Time Out*

". . . A beautifully distilled piece of work. Its brevity cannot disguise its depth, indeed it emphasises it . . . This is a beautifully-assured novella." *Herald*

"Faber shows yet again that he is *sui generis*, a tall tale-teller who despite many misleading comparisons – Kelman? Welsh? Gray? – is in a school of one." *Sunday Herald*

"This marks Faber's evolution into a writer with tremendous skill." *Uncut*

"A wonderfully constructed and observed novella; short, succinct and significant and also, gratifyingly enough, uproariously funny." *The List*

WWW.CANONGATE.NET